DANTE'S INFERNO
A Wanderer In Hell

Alexis Brooks de Vita

DANTE'S INFERNO
A Wanderer In Hell

DOUBLE DRAGON

ISBN 978-1-78695-643-9

Double Dragon
is an imprint of
Fiction4All

This Edition Published 2021
Fiction4All
www.fiction4all.com

Cover Art by Novella Serena

Canto I

Halfway down life's road
I found myself in a dark jungle,
lost off the straight path.

It's hard to describe
this jungle, so savage and harsh and strong
that just thinking about it again scares me!

Death is only a little more bitter;
but to tell you about the good I found there
I have to tell you what else I discovered.

I don't know how I got there;
I was so out of it
when I wandered off the right road.

But then I was at the foot of a hill,
there at the end of the valley
where fear shot through my heart;

I looked up to its shoulders
wearing rays of light from that planet
that leads everyone on every path right.

The fear calmed,
in the lake of my heart where all
that night I'd been so stressed.

And like people out of breath
who rise from the sea to the shore
and then turn back to the dangerous water,

so my mind, still running away,
turned to look back
where no other person had ever gotten through alive.

I rested my tired body
and started again up the desert hillside,
the foot lowest down always on firmest ground.

And there, at the bottom of the highest point,
a leopard lightweight and very fast,
its fur all spotted,

wouldn't back off from me
and blocked my path,
so I kept turning to go back down.

It was early in the morning,
and the sun rose with those stars
that were with it when divine love

first stirred up beautiful things;
I felt I could still hope for the best,
despite that furred cat

because of the hour and the sweet season;
until the fear that struck me
at the sight of a lion.

He came at me
with his head high and crazy hungry,
so the air itself trembled.

And a she-wolf, all bony,
ravenous in her skinniness
—so many people live hungry—

so weighed me down
with fear at the sight of her
that I lost hope of reaching the top.

And like the man who's happy to win,
but when the time comes to lose, he does it
all crying and sad,

that's how the restless beast
coming at me, little by little,
drove me down to where the sun is silent.

While I went down low,
to my eyes was offered the sight of
a figure in the long silence.

When I saw him in the huge desert,
"Have pity on me," I shouted to him,
"whatever you are, ghost or real man!"

He answered me: "Not a man, though I was a man,
my parents from Lombardy,
both from Mantua.

I was born at the end of the reign of King Julius
and lived in Rome under good King Augustus
with false and lying gods.

I was a poet and sang of

Aeneas who came from Troy
after Ilium burned down.

But you, why are you going back to so much pain?
Why not just go up this delightful hill
of joy?"

"So you're that Virgil who is a fountain
of speech like a river?"
I asked, shamefaced.

"Honored light of poets,
value the long study and great love
that made me search your volume.

You are my teacher and my author,
the one whose beautiful style I took
that brought me honor.

You see the beast that forced me back;
help me, famous wise man,
because she makes my blood tremble in my veins."

"It would be better for you to go another way,"
he said when he saw my tears,
"if you want to get out of this crazy jungle;

that beast that makes you want to scream
doesn't let anyone pass,
but stops him and kills him;

her nature is so evil
she never satisfies her desire,

and after she feeds she's hungrier than ever.

She mates with lots of animals
and will keep on, until the one
will come who'll make her die in pain.

He won't feast on earth and wealth
but on wisdom, love and virtue,
and his nation will be between Messiahs.

He'll save humble Italy
that virgin Cammilla died for,
Euralyus and Turnus and Niso, who died of their wounds.

He'll hunt for her in every town
until he's sent her back to Hell,
where jealousy set her loose.

So I think you should follow me,
and I'll be your guide
and take you to a place that lasts forever,

where you'll hear desperate cries,
see ancient spirits suffer
as if they're crying for the Second Death,

and you'll see those content
to burn, because they hope to
be with the blessed.

When you want to rise up there,
I'll leave you with a soul more worthy than I am,
when I go.

9

The ruler up there,
because I rebelled against his laws,
doesn't want me in his city.

He rules everywhere;
here's his city and there's his throne;
his chosen ones are happy!"

I said to him: "Poet, I ask you
for the sake of that god you didn't know,
help me escape this harm and worse,

lead me where you've talked about going,
so I can see St. Peter's gate
and those people you say are so sad."
He moved, and I kept behind him.

Canto II

Day was going, and the brown air
pulled the earth's souls
from their fatigue; and I was the only one who

seemed to struggle
to face that pitiful path
that memory brings back clearly.

Muses, great genius, help me;
mind that wrote down what I saw,
show your worth.

I started: "Poet who guides me,
see if I'm strong enough,
before you trust me to this highway.

You say Aeneas
became immortal
while living.

But, if God
showed him such grace,
to raise him up

would not seem wrong to a thinking man;
Rome and its empire
gave birth to the heavenly empire,

which, to tell the truth,
is the sacred throne
of great Peter's successors.

On this journey,
your praise
inspired his victory and the Pope's robes.

Christ went there
to bring back proof of our faith
as the first step in our salvation.

But why should I go there? Who says it's okay?
I'm not Aeneas, and I'm not Paul;
No one thinks I'm good enough for this.

If I go,
I'm afraid this might be crazy.
You're wise; you understand what I'm trying to say."

Like one who changes his mind
and second-guesses himself
and gives up,

I was on that dark coast,
because thinking too much
made me doubt what I'd started to do so quickly.

"If I understand you,"
responded that generous soul,
"your soul is cowardly;

it often afflicts a man
and turns him away from doing what is good,
the way an animal fears what's in the shadows.

To free you from fear,
I'll tell you what I saw and what I heard
when I first felt sorry for you.

I was with the souls suspended in Limbo,
and a beautiful, blessed woman called me,
and I asked her what I could do for her.

Her eyes were brighter than a star;
she said in a soft smooth
angel's voice,

'Oh, Mantuan gentleman spirit,
famous in the world
for as long as the world will last,

my unlucky friend
stopped on the desert slope,
and now he turns back, scared;

I'm afraid he's so lost
that I'm too late to help him,
from what I hear in Heaven.

Go, and with your golden words
and skills,
help him and console me.

I'm Beatrice, asking you to go;
I come from a place I want to go back to;
love sent me and makes me speak to you.

When I'm before my Lord

I'll praise you to him.'
Then she was silent, and I started speaking:

'Oh, lady whose virtue
makes the human species better
than the heavens,

I'm so pleased to do what you ask
that, if I'd already done it, I'd be too late;
just let me know what you want.

But tell me why you
descended to earth
from the great place you want so much to go back to.'

'Since you want to know,
I'll tell you,' she said,
'why I'm not afraid to come in here.

We should only fear
what has the power to hurt us;
nothing else is scary.

I'm made by God's mercy so
that your misery doesn't touch me,
and these fires can't harm me.

Heaven's gentle lady is so compassionate
that she lets me send you to him,
holding back judgment.

She called St. Lucia
and said: "Now your faithful one

needs you."

Lucia, enemy of cruelty,
came to me,
sitting near Rachel.

She said: "Beatrice, the true God's praise,
why don't you help the man who loved you so much
that he got out of the vulgar crowd for you?

Don't you hear his cries;
don't you see him fighting death
at the river where the sea is lost?"

Never were men so quick
to seek their gain or escape their harm
as I was, after those words were spoken.

I came here from my sacred place
trusting in your honest speech
that honors you and those who hear it.'

After she reasoned with me,
her eyes bright with tears, she turned away,
making me hurry here even faster.

And I came to you as she wanted:
I saved you from the beast
that blocked your short way up the mountain.

Then: what? Why, why do you stay;
why is there so much cowardice in your heart?
Why are you not more straightforward and confident?

When three blessed ladies
look out for you in the court of Heaven,
and I promise you so much good?"

As little flowers frozen at night
bend and close, then when the sun whitens them,
they stand and open on their stems,

so did I in my tired virtue;
so much good poured into my heart,
that I began like a determined person:

"How she pitied me to help me!
And you were such a gentleman to obey so quickly
the true words she spoke!

Your words
have made my heart want to go,
and I've gone back to my first decision.

Let's go, because we both want the same thing:
you lead, my boss and teacher."
I said this to him; and he moved on,
and I entered the deep dangerous path.

Canto III

"Through me go to the sorrowful city,
through me go to eternal pain,
through me go among the lost people.

Justice moved my maker in Heaven;
I was made by power divine,
consummate wisdom and primal love.

Before me was nothing not eternal,
and I will be eternally.
Leave behind you every hope, you who enter me."

Those words in dark colors
I saw written above a gate;
I said: "Teacher, their meaning is ominous."

And he said to me, like a person who understands:
"Here you must let go of every suspicion;
every cowardice must be killed.

We've come to the place where I told you
that you'll see people in pain
who've lost their right minds."

He put his hand on mine;
with a soft look that comforted me,
he led me into secret things.

Here sighs, cries and loud wailing
resounded in the starless air,
so that I too started to shed tears.

Strange languages, horrible sounds,
anguished words, tones of rage,
voices high and faint, hands beating

in a tumult, spinning
in that atmosphere untouched by time,
like sand swirling.

And I with my head wrapped in error
said: "Teacher, what do I hear?
and who are these people overcome by pain?"

And he to me: "This is the miserable state
of those sad souls
who lived without blame and without praise.

They mix with that wicked crowd
of angels who didn't rebel
and who weren't faithful to God, but held out.

Heaven throws them out to spare its beauty,
and the depths of Hell don't want
their rulers to lord it over these."

And I: "Teacher, what grief
is theirs that they mourn so hard?"
He responded: "I'll tell you.

They have no hope of death,
and their blind life brings them so low,
they envy any other fate.

18

The world knows nothing of them;
pity and justice ignore them:
don't reason with them, but look at them and pass on."

And I looked, saw a flag
running round so fast
it couldn't stop;

and behind it came so long a line
of people I would not have believed
death could have undone so many.

I recognized some,
saw and knew the shadow of him
whose cowardice made his great refusal.

I understood and was sure
that this was that evil gang
God doesn't like and neither do his enemies.

These wretches, who never really lived,
were naked and stung
by fat flies and wasps.

Blood streaked down their faces,
mixed with tears, and pooled at their feet
with the worms.

I looked past
and saw people at the bank of a great river;
and I said: "Teacher, let me know

who these are, and what

makes them so ready to pass,
as it seems to me in this dim light."

And he to me: "These things you'll know
when we stop
by that sad river Acheron," the River of Woe.

Then with shamed eyes downcast,
fearing what I said had bothered him,
I didn't speak again until we got to the river.

And there, coming toward us in a boat,
an old man, hair white with age,
shouted: "Curse you, depraved souls!

Give up hope of seeing Heaven:
I've come to take you to the other shore,
into the eternal shadows, the heat and cold.

And you there, living soul,
Get away from those dead."
But when he saw I didn't go away,

he said: "By another way, other ports,
you'll see a shore, not here, where you can pass:
lighter wood will have to carry you."

And my boss to him: "Charon, don't crucify yourself:
one does what one can where one can
as one wants to, and asks nothing more."

That quieted the woolly jaws
of the navigator of that livid swamp,

20

with flaming circles around his eyes.

But those souls, sad and naked,
paled and their teeth chattered
as soon as they heard his crude words.

They blasphemed God and their parents,
the human race the place the time the seed
of their beginning and their birth.

Then they stepped together,
crying hard, to the cursed shore
that waits for every man who doesn't fear God.

Demon Charon, with coal eyes
signaled them, gathered them,
beat with his oar anyone who slowed.

Just as autumn lifts away leaves
one after another, until the branch
sees its spoils on the earth,

in the same way, Adam's bad seed
threw themselves from that shore one by one,
like a falcon called to flight.

So they go over dark waves
ahead; yet, before they descend,
more have gathered here.

"My son," said the courteous teacher,
"those who die in God's anger
come here from every country;

and they are ready to cross the river,
for divine justice pushes them,
so fear becomes desire.

A good soul never crosses here;
so, if Charon protests about you,
now you can understand what he means."

Having said this, the dark countryside
trembled so hard that fear
bathed my head in sweat.

From the weeping earth rose wind
that swept red light
and left me senseless;
and I fell like a man knocked out by sleep.

Canto IV

In my head broke the sound
of thunder, so I shook
like a person forced awake;

my rested eye looked around,
raised, and fixed its gaze
so I might know where I was.

I found myself
in the abyss of suffering
where infinite anguish gathered,

dark and deep and cloudy,
so that, straining to see the bottom,
I could make out nothing.

"Now we're going down into the blind world,"
began the poet, all colorless.
"I'll be first and you second."

And I, noticing his color,
said: "How will I come, if you're scared,
you who comfort me?"

And he to me: "The anguish of the people
down there paints my face
with pity you mistake for fear.

Let's go, for a long road waits."
So he went, and I entered
the first circle of the abyss.

Here, according to what I could hear,
were no cries but sighs
and the eternally trembling air,

that came from pain without martyrdom
of the many
children and women and men.

The good teacher to me: "You don't ask
what spirits these are that you see?
I want you to know before you go on,

they didn't sin; if they have merit,
it's not enough because they weren't baptized,
denied entry into the faith you believe in;

and if they lived before Christianity,
they worshipped God poorly.
I'm among these.

For these defects and no other fault,
we're lost, and for these offenses
we live in hopeless longing."

Great pain took my heart when I understood,
for I knew important people
were suspended in this Limbo.

"Tell me, my teacher, tell me, sir,"
I said, wanting to be certain
of that faith that conquers error:

24

"did anyone ever leave, by his own merit
or someone else's, and become blessed?"
And he, who understood my secret question,

responded: "I was new, in this state,
when I saw a powerful man come
crowned with victory.

He brought out the spirits of our first parent,
of his son Abel and Noah,
of Moses the obedient lawgiver,

Abraham the patriarch and David the king,
Israel with his father and sons,
and Rachel, whom he was faithful to,

and lots of others, and blessed them.
I want you to know that, before these,
human spirits weren't saved."

We didn't stop walking as he talked,
but passed through a jungle
thick with spirits.

We hadn't gone far from where I'd slept
when I saw a fire
light the dark hemisphere.

We were still some way from it,
but not so far I couldn't tell
that honorable people were at that place.

"Honored one of science and art,

why are these honorable ones
set apart from the others?"

He said to me: "Their honor,
famous in your life up there,
is seen favorably in Heaven and promotes them."

I heard a voice say:
"Highly honored poet,
the ghost returns that had departed!"

The voice quieted,
and I saw four great shadows approach us,
neither sad nor pleased.

The good teacher began to speak:
"Look at him with his sword in hand,
who comes before the other three:

he's Homer, poet king;
Horace the satirist;
third, Ovid; last Lucan.

Each is,
in the name the one voice called,
honoring me, and all poets."

I saw the beautiful school
of the lord of the highest song
that soars like an eagle.

After they talked,
they turned to me with signs of greeting,

26

and my teacher smiled;

and more honor they showed me
by making me one of their crowd,
the sixth among them.

So we went toward the light
speaking of beautiful things I can't repeat here,
as it was right to speak of them there.

We came to the bottom of a noble castle,
seven times circled by high walls,
defended around by a lovely stream.

This we crossed like hard land;
seven gates I entered with these wise men
until we reached a fresh green field.

People were there with slow, grave eyes,
with great authority in their bearing;
they spoke little, with smooth voices.

We moved to one side,
an open space, high and well lit,
where we could see everyone.

Straight ahead over the green,
great spirits showed themselves to me
so that, seeing them, I felt wonderful.

I saw Electra with her people,
and recognized Hector and Aeneas among them,
armed Caesar with his gryphon eyes.

I saw Cammilla and Pantasilea;
off to one side the Latino king
sitting with his daughter Lavinia.

I saw Brutus who chased off Tarquino,
Lucrezia, Julia, Marcia, and Cornelia;
And alone, aside, I saw Saladín.

I looked up a little higher,
and saw the teacher of the wise
sitting with his philosophical family.

Everyone watched him; everyone honored him.
I saw Socrates and Plato
in front of the others and nearest him;

Democritus who leaves the world to chance,
Diogenes, Anaxagoras and Tale,
Empedocles, Heraclitus, and Zeno;

I saw the good collector of the nature of things,
Dioscorides; and I saw Orpheus,
Cicero Linus and moral Seneca.

Euclid the geometer and Ptolemy,
Hippocrates, Avicenna and Galen,
Averois who wrote the great commentary.

I can't list all of them
because I'm pursued by my story
and telling lessens it.

28

The group of six loses two;
my wise boss takes me another way,
out of the quiet, into the trembling air,
and I come to a place without any light.

Canto V

So I went down from the first circle
to the second, which surrounds
more pain, pushed to anguish.

There stands horrible Minos, growling:
he examines the guilty at the gate,
judges and sends them off with his coils.

When the bad soul
comes to him, it confesses all;
and that knower of sins

sees what place in Hell is for this one,
circles his tail around himself as many times
as how many circles down the soul must be sent.

There is always a crowd in front of him
going to judgment;
they speak they listen and then are thrown down.

"You who come to this painful place,"
said Minos to me when he saw me,
leaving off his important job,

"watch out how you come in here and who you trust;
don't be fooled by how easy it is to get in here!"
And my boss said to him, "Why all the yelling?

Don't get in the way of his fated trip:
it is willed where what can be
is what is wanted, and nothing more can be asked."

Now I hear screams
of pain; I've come
to where crying pounds at me.

I've come to a place where light is muted,
roaring like the sea in a storm,
battered by crosswinds.

The hellish storm that never stops
carries off spirits,
swinging beating upsetting them.

When they are caught up in the devastation,
they scream complain and cry,
blaspheming the divine good.

I understood that this is the torment
of sinners of the flesh,
who suppress reason.

And as little wings
in the cold carry large full flocks of birds,
so the storm did to these evil spirits:

here, there, down, up it takes them;
no hope ever comforts them,
nor rest or less punishment.

And as birds sing their sad songs,
a long line in the air,
so I saw them come, bringing their misery,

shadows carried by that storm;
so I said: "Teacher, who are these people
whipped by the black air?"

"The first of them
you would know about," he said to me,
"was empress of many languages.

Lust ruined her;
she made it law,
to free her own behavior from blame.

She is Semiramis,
Nino's wife and successor
in the land ruled by the Sultan.

Here is the woman who killed herself for love
and broke faith with Sicheo's ashes;
there's lustful Cleopatra.

You see Helen, who caused so many
lost years, and you see great Achilles,
who fought love at the end.

You see Paris, Tristan," and he showed me
thousands of shadows, pointed and named them
that love had sent from life.

When I heard my professor
name the ancient ladies and gentlemen,
pity took hold of me, and I almost fainted.

I started to say: "Poet, I would like

to speak with those two going by together,
so light in the wind."

He said to me: "You'll see when they
get closer to us; if you ask them
for the sake of the love that carries them, they'll come."

As soon as the wind drove them to us,
I called: "Tired souls,
come talk to us, if no one says you can't!"

As doves called by desire,
wings raised at the sweet nest,
come through the air in flight,

these left Dido's crowd,
coming to us through the evil air,
so strong was my loving call.

"Oh gracious kind living thing
who comes visiting through this lost air
those of us who painted the world with our blood,

if the king of the universe were our friend,
we would ask him to give you peace
because you took pity on our perversity.

What you'd like to hear and speak about,
we'll hear and speak about with you,
while the wind, as it is doing, quiets down.

The land where I was born
sits at the shore where the Po River flows

peacefully.

Love, so flammable in a gentle heart,
took hold of this beautiful man
who was taken from me; the way it happened still upsets
me.

Love, that no one loved can pardon from loving,
took such strong hold of me with his pleasantness
that, as you see, he still hasn't left me.

Love carried us away to one death.
The bottom of Hell waits for the man who ended our life."
The words carried from them to us.

When I understood these distressed souls,
I lowered my head
until the poet said: "What are you thinking?"

When I answered, I started with: "What
sweet thoughts, how much desire
brought them to such a sorrowful end!"

Then I turned to them
and said: "Francesca, your suffering
makes me weep with sadness and pity.

But tell me: in the time of sweet sighs,
how and in what way did love
make you know your doubtful desires?"

And she said to me: "No greater suffering
than to remember happy times

in misery; and your professor knows this.

But if knowing the first root
of our love attracts you,
I will tell you as one who cries and talks.

We were reading one day with delight
of Lancelot seized by love;
we were alone and unsuspecting.

Our eyes held each other
while reading, and our faces drained of color;
but only one point defeated us.

When we read that the smile he wanted so much
was kissed by such a lover,
this man, who will never be taken from me,

kissed my mouth, all trembling.
The book was a pimp and so was the man who wrote it:
that day we read no further."

While one spirit said this,
the other cried, so that pity
overwhelmed me as if I had died.
And I fell like a dead body falls.

Canto VI

When my mind came back to me, after it shut down
for pity of those two cousins
whose sadness totally confused me,

new torments and the newly tormented
I see all around me, as I move
or turn or look.

I am in the third circle, of eternal rain,
cursed, cold and heavy;
never changing.

Huge hail, filthy water and snow
back and forth in the cloudy air;
the earth stinks where this lands.

Cerberus, cruel strange creature
with three dog throats, barks
over the mired people.

His eyes are red, his beard oily and darkened,
his gut huge, claws on his hands;
he claws the spirits, skins and splits them in four.

They howl in the rain like dogs;
they shield one side with the other,
rolling, the condemned wretches.

When Cerberus saw us, the great worm,
his mouths opened and showed his fangs;
all of him quivered.

And my boss reached out his hands,
snatched up mud, and with fists full
threw it into the hungry throats.

What is that barking dog
that it quiets as it chews its meal,
focused only on devouring it,

those ugly faces
of the demon Cerberus that thunders
on the souls so they wish they were deaf?

We passed over shadows
under the heavy rain and stepped
on the vanity that seems to make them persons.

They all stretched out on the ground,
except for one who sat up as soon as
it saw us pass in front of it.

"Oh you, brought through this Hell,"
it said to me, "remember me, if you know:
you were, before I was unmade, made."

And I said to him: "Your suffering,
Maybe, pulls you out of my mind,
so it doesn't seem to me I've ever seen you.

But tell me who you are, put in such pain
in this place, doing such penance
that, if there's greater, nothing's worse."

And he to me: "Your city, so full
of envy that the sack's spilling,
held me in serene life.

You citizens called me Ciacco:
for the damaging guilt of gluttony,
as you see, I'm facedown in this rain.

And I, sad soul, am not alone;
all these punishments
are for the same guilt." He didn't say another word.

I answered him: "Ciacco, your distress
weighs me down and makes me want to weep;
but tell me, if you know, what will become

of the citizens of that divided city?
Is anyone there fair-minded? And tell me
why so much in-fighting screws it up."

He said to me: "After a long feud,
there will be blood, and the peasants
will hunt down the others and hurt them.

But this
in three suns' time, and the other will overcome
by force.

For a long time,
they'll weigh down the other
with crying and shame.

Two men are fair-minded, and no one listens to them;

arrogance, jealousy and greed
burn in their hearts."

Here ended his upsetting sounds.
And I to him: "Teach me more,
and give me more of what you have to say.

Farinata and Tegghiaio, so deserving,
Jacob Rusticucci, Arrigo and The Fly,
and the others who mean well,

tell me where they are and what they're up to;
I really want to know
if they're finding Heaven sweet or if Hell is making them
bitter."

And he: "They are among darker souls;
different sins weigh them down to the depths:
if you go down that far, you'll see them.

But when you're back in the sweet world,
I beg you to remind others of me;
I won't tell you any more or answer you anymore."

Then his straight gaze turned inward;
he looked toward me a little longer and then bent his
head;
he tumbled back in among the rest of the blind.

My boss said to me: "He won't wake
from that sleep until the sound of angels' trumpets,
when he'll see the enemy power;

each will see again his sad tomb,
put back on his flesh and shape,
hear that eternal sound."

We passed through that disgusting mix
of shadows and rain with slow steps,
talking about life in the future;

so I said, "Teacher, these torments
will be worse after the great judgment,
or not so bad, or the same?"

And he to me: "Refer back to your science,
which says that the more perfect a thing is,
the more it feels what is good and also suffers.

Even though these condemned people
will never be truly perfect,
they'll be closer to it than they are now, while they're
waiting."

We moved around that street,
speaking of more than I'll repeat;
we came to the point of descent;
here we found Pluto, the great enemy.

Canto VII

"Holy Father Satan, Holy Father Satan, the First!"
started up Pluto in his scratchy voice;
and that wise gentleman, who knew everything,

said to comfort me: "Don't give in
to your fear; whatever power he has,
he can't turn us back from climbing down this rock."

Then he turned to that bigmouth
and said: "Quiet, cursed wolf!
may your rage eat your insides!

This descent into sin isn't without permission:
it's wanted on high, where Michael
beat down that arrogant uprising."

As the wind swells sails
that tumble when the mast snaps,
so fell to earth that cruel creature.

So we went down into the fourth void,
down the sorrowful path
that held all the evil of the universe.

Oh, God's justice! who piles up
such punishments and pains as I saw?
And why does sin wear us down like this?

As waves above Charybdis
crash against each other,
so the people here line-dance.

Here I saw more people than anywhere,
everywhere, shouting,
shoving weights.

They crashed into each other,
and each turned back,
screaming, "Why hoard? Why waste?"

So they turned in their circle
from every side to the opposite point,
shrieking the same line;

then each turned, once they met,
halfway through the circle to the next crash.
And I, my heart almost stabbed through,

said, "My teacher, show me
who these people are, and if those with shaved heads
were clergy, to our left."

And he to me: "All of them had near-sighted
minds in the first life,
and didn't measure their spending.

They bay this clearly
when they come to the two points of the circle
where opposite sins scatter them.

In those hairless clergy,
popes and cardinals,
greed was supreme."

And I: "Teacher,
I should recognize some
immersed in these evils."

And he to me: "Useless thought;
their thoughtless life
covered them with too much filth to figure them out.

These two groups will clash forever;
these will rise from the grave
with their fists closed, these with shaved heads.

Bad giving and bad keeping took a seductive world
from them, and put them in this gang fight;
whatever it was, I have no nice words for it.

Now you see, son, what a punch line
Fortune makes of our belongings,
with human people the joke;

all the gold under the moon,
ever, couldn't give one of these tired souls
rest."

"My teacher," I said "tell me more:
this Fortune you told me about,
what is it, that it hangs on to the world's goods?"

And he to me: "Stupid creatures,
what ignorance messes you around!
Swallow my judgment of it.

The one whose wisdom transcends all

made the heavens to
shine from every place to everywhere,

spreading light.
So earthly splendor
he ordained to go,

vain gifts, in time
from people to people of different blood,
beyond human ability to control it;

so one people rules and another languishes,
following his judgment,
hidden like a snake in the grass.

Your wisdom can't resist her:
she sees, judges and rules
like any other god.

She changes ceaselessly,
fast,
endlessly.

She's crucified
by those who should praise her,
blaming her wrongly and badly;

but she is blessed and doesn't hear:
with other primal beasts, happy,
she turns her wheel.

Now we come down to the greatest suffering;

every star falls that was rising
when I got started; we can't hang around."

We retraced the circle to the other shore
over a fountain that boiled and returned
through the way it came.

Water darker than indigo;
we, on its somber waves,
made our weird descent

to the swamp called Styx, the River of Hatred,
this sad stream,
malignant grey slopes.

And I, staring hard,
saw muddy people in that plain,
naked, angry.

They hit each other not just with hands,
but head and chest and feet,
and shred each other with teeth.

The good teacher said: "Son, now see
the souls of those anger defeated;
believe

under the water, people breathe
and bubble the water at the top,
as your eye tells you.

Trapped in the slime, they say: 'We were sad
in sweet air and happy sun,

sluggish inside;

now we are sad in the black bog.'
This bubbles in their throats
for they can't speak a word."

So we circled the filthy swamp
in a great arc between dry bank and bog,
an eye turned on those who swallowed mud.
And we came to the foot of a tower.

Canto VIII

I'll say, going on, that before
we were at the foot of the tower,
our eyes had seen at its summit

two flames
and another, far off, signaling,
that could hardly be seen.

I turned to that sea of knowledge
and said: "What is this saying? and what answer
from that other fire? and who is doing this?"

And he to me: "Over the stinking waves
you can make out what's waiting for you,
if the swamp's miasma doesn't hide it."

A bow never shot any arrow
faster through the air
than I saw a small boat

come toward us through the water,
under one pilot
who shouted: "Now I've got you, foul soul!"

"Phlegyas, Phlegyas, you shout into the void,"
said my boss, "this time;
you won't have us longer than it takes to cross."

Like someone who hears a huge trick
has been played on him and seethes,
Phlegyas smothered his anger.

My boss got in the boat
and had me get in after him;
after I got in, it seemed full.

As soon as my boss and I were in the bark,
the ancient prow cuts
deep in the water.

While we crossed the dead swamp,
something covered in mud came at me
and said: "Who are you to come here before your time?"

And I to it: "Maybe I came, but I'm not staying;
but who are you, who turned out so hideous?"
It said: "You see I'm one who cries."

And I to it: "With crying and suffering,
cursed spirit, you stay;
I know you, even with all your filth."

It held out both hands to the boat;
the teacher pushed it away,
saying: "Away with the other dogs!"

He hugged me around my neck
kissed my face and said: "Disdainful soul,
blessed is the woman who was pregnant with you!

In the world this person was arrogant;
no generosity decorates his memory,
so his soul is furious.

How many who think they're great as kings
will be here like pigs in the mud,
leaving behind horrible disgrace!"

And I: "Teacher, I'd really like
to see it suffocate in that broth
before we leave the lake."

And he to me: "Before
you see the shore, you'll be satisfied;
what you want deserves to be had."

Soon I saw
the muddy people rip him to shreds,
may God be praised and thanked.

All screamed, "Get Filippo Argenti!"
and that bizarre Florentine spirit
turned on himself with his own teeth.

I leave him here and say no more about him;
but mourning in my ears
opened my eyes straight ahead.

The good teacher said: "Now, son,
we near the city called Dis
with its grave citizens, its great legion."

And I: "Teacher, already its mosques
ignite between the walls
and glow red as if pulled from fire."

And he said to me: "Eternal

fire burning inside them shows red,
as you see, in the depths of Hell."

We reached the moats
like valleys in the inconsolable earth;
the walls seemed made of iron.

We circled wide
and came to where the powerful ferryman
shouted: "Out; here is the entrance!"

I saw more than a thousand at the gates, fallen
like rain from Heaven, who furiously
were saying: "Who is that, not dead,

who goes through the kingdom of the dead?"
And my wise teacher made a sign
to speak with them secretly.

They shut down their great disdain a little to
say: "You come alone, and let him go,
who so wanted to come into this kingdom.

Let him return alone along his crazy way,
if he can; you'll stay,
you who escorted him through the dark."

Think, reader, of how upset I was
at the sound of those cursed words
because I didn't think I'd ever get back.

"Oh my dear boss, who more than seven
times made me sure and safe

from dangers all around me,

don't leave me," I said, "so undone;
if they won't let us through,
let's find our way back together, right now."

But the lord who had led me
said to me: "Don't be afraid; our passage
can't be blocked by anyone: by such a one it was granted.

But you wait here for me;
feed and comfort your tired spirit with good hope;
I won't leave you in this lowdown world."

He goes and abandons me,
sweet father, and I am left in doubt,
yes and no fighting in my head.

I couldn't hear what he presented to them;
but he wasn't with them long
before they all ran back inside.

Our adversaries shut the gates
in my boss's face who, outside,
came back to me with slow steps.

Eyes to the ground, brow stripped
of boldness, he sighed to me:
"Who denied me these sorry houses!"

And he said to me: "You, because I'm upset,
don't worry; I'll win this fight,
whatever they're up to in there.

51

This nastiness of theirs isn't new;
I've already used their secret gate
that doesn't lock.

Over this one you saw the writing of death;
and already someone descends through it,
coming through the circles without a guide,
for whom the land opens."

Canto IX

The color my cowardice painted me,
seeing my boss turn back,
made him hold himself in.

Listening attentively, he stopped;
for the eye couldn't see far
in the black air and thick fog.

"We still have to win the tussle,"
he started, "otherwise. . . But such help was offered.
It's taking so long for someone to get here!"

I saw that he had covered up
what he started to say with something else that came to
him,
words very different from the first ones;

all the same, what he said scared me;
maybe I understood his broken phrase
to mean worse than it seemed.

"In this depth of the sad shell,
does anyone ever get here from the first level,
where the only loss is hope?"

I questioned; and he: "I rarely
meet," he said, "any of us
who make this trip that I'm on.

I did come down here another time,
conjured up by that crude Erichtho

who could call spirits back to their bodies.

I hadn't been stripped of my body for long
when she made me enter through that wall
to bring a spirit from Judas's circle.

That place is lowest and darkest
and the furthest from Heaven that encloses all;
I know the way quite well, be assured.

This swamp with its great stink
encircles the sorrowful city,
and we can't get in without rage."

He said more, but I don't remember it;
but my eye was drawn
to the high tower's broken peak

where suddenly rose
three hellish bloodstained Furies,
shaped and moving like women

with green hydras belting their waists;
serpents for hair
crowned their fierce heads.

And he, who knew well the maids
of the queen of eternal mourning,
"Look," he said to me, "the ferocious Furies.

That's Megaera on the left;
the one weeping on the right is Alecto;
Tisiphone is in the middle;" and he was silent.

With their nails they tore at their chests;
they beat themselves and shrieked;
I anxiously drew closer to the poet.

"Come Medusa: we'll turn him to stone,"
they said looking down;
"it was a mistake not to avenge the assault of Theseus."

"Turn your back and keep your eyes closed;
if the Gorgon shows herself, and you see her,
you'll have no chance of going back up."

So said the teacher; and he
turned me, and not trusting my hands,
with his own closed my eyes.

You who have sane minds,
look at the doctrine
veiled by these strange verses.

And already over the turbid waves,
a chaotic, fearful sound was coming
shaking both shores,

like a wind
suddenly strong
blasting the forest with its full might,

the branches shattered, beaten and carried off;
blowing dirt before it,
driving off herd and shepherd.

He uncovered my eyes and said: "Now turn
your face up across that ancient bog
to the harsh smoke."

Like frogs before their enemy
flee through water
until they reach land,

I saw more than a thousand destroyed souls
flee in front of one who stepped
across the Styx, the River of Hatred, with dry feet.

He cleared the greasy air from his face,
wiping often with his left hand,
as if only that anguish tired him.

I was well aware that he was sent from Heaven,
and I turned to the teacher; he made a sign
to keep quiet and kneel.

How full of disdain he seemed to me!
He came to the gate and with a wand
opened it, so there was no resistance.

"Hunted from Heaven, hated people,"
he said at the horrible threshold,
"where do you get this contrariness?

Why do you resist that will
that will never be moved,
and so many times has made your pain greater?

What do you get out of resisting your fate?

Your Cerberus, you should well remember,
still carries the scar on his neck."

He turned to go back the awful way he'd come,
without a word for us, for he seemed
like a man eaten up by other cares

than those of the men in front of him;
we moved,
secure in his holy words.

We entered without any more fighting;
and I, in my great desire to look
at the condition of that fortress,

as soon as I was inside
saw a vast countryside
full of suffering and torment.

As at Arles where the Rhone stagnates,
as at Pola near Carnaro
that closes Italy and bathes its borders,

tombs make the place uneven;
everywhere
seemed bitter;

flames scattered,
the graves lit and burning,
hotter than iron at the forge.

All the graves' lids were held open,
and from them poured out hard sobs

from the miserable ones, suffering.

And I: "Teacher, who are these people
who, buried in those caskets,
make us hear their sorrowful sighs?"

And he to me: "Here are the arch-heretics
with their followers of every sect, and many
more fill these tombs than you would believe.

Like is buried with like here,
and the monuments burn."
Then he turned to the right,
and we went out between the sufferers and the high walls.

Canto X

Now down a secret street,
between the wall and the suffering people,
my teacher and I, at his shoulder.

"Highest virtue, through impious twists
turning me," I started, "as you like,
talk to me, satisfy what I want.

The people laid out in these tombs,
can we look at them? All
the lids are lifted, and no one's on guard."

And he to me: "All will be closed
when they come back from Jehosaphat
with the bodies they left up there.

Around here is the cemetery
of Epicurus and his followers,
who make out that the soul dies with the body.

But your question
will soon be satisfied in here,
and that wish you're still hiding from me."

And I: "Good boss, I don't keep
anything in my heart from you except to speak little,
as you've advised me."

"Tuscan going through the fiery city
alive and speaking so honestly,
if you don't mind, stay here.

The way you talk makes it very clear
that you're from that noble fatherland
that I may have attacked unfairly."

Suddenly this sound came out
of one of the caskets; and I went,
scared, a little closer to my boss.

And he said to me: "Turn around! What are you doing?
Look at Farinata rising:
you can see him from the waist up."

I'd already fixed my gaze on his;
and his chest and face surged up
as if in great spite of Hell.

My boss's lively hands quickly
pushed me past the tombs toward him,
saying: "Your words count."

When I was at the foot of his tomb,
he looked at me a little and then, disdainfully,
he asked me: "Who were your ancestors?"

I really wanted to obey
and hid nothing from him, but was open with him;
he raised his eyebrows a little in surprise

and said: "They were fiercely against
me, my people and my party,
so much so that I had to banish them twice."

60

"If you scattered them, they returned from everywhere,"
I responded to him, "the first time and the second;
your people haven't learned that skill very well."

Then rose from the opened tomb
a shadow, down to its chin;
I think it rose up on its knees.

It looked around me as if
to see if someone was with me;
and then when its suspicion was dead,

crying, it said: "If you go through this blind
prison with your high genius,
where's my son? and why isn't he with you?"

And I to him: "I'm not coming on my own:
the guy who's waiting for me over there is taking me;
maybe your Guido disdained him."

His words and his punishment
had already told me his name;
so my answer was loaded.

He stood up and shouted: "What?
Did you use past tense? Isn't he alive anymore?
Doesn't sweet light shine on his eyes?"

When he realized I hesitated
to answer,
he fell and disappeared.

But that other great one who had

made me stop didn't wait quietly
or move his neck or bend;

continuing to speak,
"If they had that skill," he said, "they learned it badly,
and that torments me more than this bed.

But fifty times
the face of the lady who reigns here will light again,
and you'll know what a burden that skill is.

And if you ever go back to the sweet world,
tell me: why are those people so
against mine in every law?"

Then I to him: "The slaughter and great bloodshed
that colored the Arbia red
make us say such prayers in our temple."

After he shook his head, sighing,
"I wasn't alone," he said, "and certainly
wouldn't have done this with the others without reason.

But I was alone, there
when all of them agreed to destroy Florence,
and I was the one who spoke up bald-faced in its
defense."

"So your seed may someday rest,"
I urged him, "help me untie this knot
that has tangled my senses.

If I've heard right, it seems you see

ahead of time what's coming,
but in the present, no way."

"We see, like those in bad light,
things," he said, "that are far away;
the lord's light shines that much.

As they get close or happen, everything's in vain
intellectually; and if others don't bring it to us,
we know nothing about your human state.

But you can understand that death
shuts down our consciousness at the point
that the door to the future is closed."

Then, guilty and sorry,
I said, "Now then, tell the guy who fell
that his son's still among the living;

and if just now my answer was silent,
let him know it's because I was thinking
about the error you'd solved for me."

And already my teacher called me back;
so I urged the spirit
to tell me who was with him.

He said to me: "Here more than a thousand lie
with me: in here's Frederick the second
and the Cardinal; I won't say anything about the rest."

He hid; and I turned
my steps toward the ancient poet, thinking back

on our talk that seemed hostile.

He made a move, and going on,
said to me: "Why are you so confused?"
I satisfied his curiosity.

"Keep in mind what you heard
against you," that wise man commanded me;
"and now wait here," and he raised a finger:

"when you're before the sweet ray
of the woman whose beautiful eyes see all,
you'll find out your life's journey from her."

He turned his steps left;
we left the wall and turned toward the center
along a path into a valley
whose disgusting stink rose.

Canto XI

At the extreme edge of a high cliff
of great broken rocks in a circle,
we came upon an even cruder group;

and here the horrible
stink the depths of the abyss threw up
drove us back, seeking the shelter

of a great mausoleum, where I saw written:
"I keep Pope Anastasius
who Photinus pulled from the straight path."

"We must put off going down,
so we can exhaust our sense of that sorry smell,
then we won't notice it."

The teacher said this; and I: "Some compensation,"
to him, "so the passing time won't be
lost." And he: "You'll see what I'm thinking.

My son, inside these rocks,"
he then started to say, "are three small circles
one under the other, like the ones you left behind.

They're all full of cursed spirits;
so that the sight of them might be enough for you,
understand how and why they're restrained.

Every evil hated in Heaven
ends in injury, and every such end
with force or fraud is going to bring down somebody.

Because fraud is men's own evil,
it's more displeasing to God; and so
frauds are lower down and their assault more painful.

The first circle holds all the violent;
but since violence can be done in three ways,
there are three distinct rings.

To God or to the next person one can do
violence, I mean against them or their things,
as you'll hear.

Violent death and painful wounds
can be done to the next person, and his possessions
ruined, burned, and damaged while stolen;

so murderers and those who hurt others,
those who waste and predators, all
are punished in the first ring in different groups.

A man can do violence to himself
and his goods; and in the second
ring uselessly repent

whoever deprives himself of your world,
gambles and wastes his faculties,
and cries there where he should be happy.

One can do violence to God,
denying him and cursing him in our hearts,
abusing nature and her bounty;

so the smallest ring seals
with its sign Sodom and Caorsa
and those who scorn God in their hearts and their speech.

Fraud eats at every conscience,
either of the man used who trusted
or the one whose trust was not enough.

This way of undoing breaks
the natural love bond;
so in the second circle nest

hypocrisy, flattery, magic-makers,
lies, theft and greed,
pimps, political prostitutes, and such filth.

In the other way, love is forgotten
that nature made and that
special faith creates;

in the smallest circle, the point
of the universe Dis sits on,
whoever betrays it is consumed forever."

And I: "Teacher, your reasoning is clear
enough and distinguishes
this pit and the people who possess it.

But tell me: those of the oily swamp,
driven by wind, beaten by rain,
who meet with bitter tongues,

why in the red city

are they not punished, if God is angry with them?
And if not, why are they like that?"

And he to me: "Why all this delirium?"
he said. "Where else is your
mind looking?

Don't you remember those words
with which your Ethics discusses
the three dispositions Heaven doesn't want:

incontinence, malice and mad
bestiality? And how incontinence
offends God less and attracts less blame?

If you look well at this sentence
and recall to mind who are those
up there outside doing penance,

you will see quite well why these felons
are separated, and why they are
hammered less by God's revenge."

"Sun that heals every troubled sight,
you content me when you resolve,
as, no less than knowing, doubting pleases me.

Go back a little,"
I said, "to where you said charging interest offends
divine bounty, and resolve the tangle."

"Philosophy," he said to me, "for who understands it,
notes, not only in one place,

how nature takes its course

from divine intellect and its art;
and if you understand Physics well,
you'll find, after not too many pages,

that your human skill, as much as it can,
follows, like a disciple does his teacher;
your skill is like God's grandchild.

From these two, if you remember
the beginning of Genesis, it's necessary
to earn a livelihood and advance the people;

but the interest-charger takes another way,
disrespects nature and its laws
and puts his hope in another.

But follow me now along this turn that draws me;
Pisces shines east on the horizon,
and the Great Bear lies over the northwest,
and there is the way down."

Canto XII

It was at the place where the cliff plummeted
that we went down, like the Alps;
every eye would slide away from what we saw.

Like the ruin on the side
of the Trento, the Adige,
either because of earthquake or lack of support,

from the mountain top
to the plain where the fallen rocks scattered,
there was no way down:

that's how the drop was;
and at the point of the broken chasm,
the infamy of Crete stretched out,

conceived in the false cow;
and when it saw us, it moved,
as if driven by rage inside.

My wise man shouted to him: "Maybe
you believe this is the ruler of Athens
who in the world up there put you to death?

Get away, beast, since this man doesn't come
taught by your sister,
but to see your punishments."

Like the bull that breaks free in that
moment it receives the death blow
and doesn't know how to walk, but jumps here and there,

I saw the Minotaur do;
and the cautious one shouted: "Run to the passage;
while he's furious, it's best that you get down."

And so we went down the landslide
of those stones that often moved
under my feet from the new weight.

I was already thinking; and he said: "You're thinking
maybe about this ruin, guarded
by that bestial anger I just put out.

I want you to know the other time
I came down here into lower Hell,
this rock hadn't fallen yet.

But a little before, if I'm right,
he came down who plundered
Dis in the highest circle.

Everywhere the deep foul valley
trembled, so I thought the universe
felt love, for lack of which some believe

many times the world has been driven to chaos;
and at that point this old rock,
here and everywhere, fell in on itself.

But fix your eyes on the valley that approaches
the river of blood boiling
those whose violence hurts others."

Blind greed and crazy rage,
that in this short life push us,
and in the eternal, cook us!

I saw a great moat twisted in an arc
that hugged the plain,
like my escort said;

and between the foot of the cliff and this, a file
of centaurs ran, armed with arrows,
like they used to hunt in the world.

Seeing us come down, each stopped,
and three left the squad,
choosing their bows and arrows first;

and one shouted from far off: "To what suffering
are you coming down the hill?
Tell us from where you are; if not, I draw the bow."

My teacher said: "We'll answer
Chiron right over there;
you were always quick-tempered."

Then he touched me and said: "That's Nessus,
who died for the beautiful Deianira,
and made himself his own revenge.

And that one in the middle, staring down at his chest,
is the great Chiron, who raised Achilles;
the other is Folo, so full of anger.

Thousands and thousands go around the moat,

shooting arrows at any soul that they see
come out of the blood further than guilt releases him."

We approached the fleet-footed creatures:
Chiron took an arrow and used its notch
to pull his beard back to his jaws.

When he'd uncovered his huge mouth,
he said to his companions: "Were you aware
the one in the back moves whatever he touches?

That's not what dead people's feet do."
And my good boss, at his chest
where the two natures are joined,

responded: "He's quite alive, and so isolated
I have to show him through the dark valley;
necessity makes us do this, not fun.

Someone quit singing hallelujah
to give me this new job;
he's not a thief, and I'm not an escaping soul.

But for that virtue that made me
walk down this savage street,
give us one of your men we can stick close to,

who'll show us where to cross
and carry this guy on his back,
since he's not a spirit who goes through the air."

Chiron turned to his right
and said to Nessus: "Come back, and guide them,

73

and if you meet another squadron, make them give way."

We moved on with this trustworthy escort
along the edge of the boiling red
where the boiled scream.

I saw people submerged to the eyebrows;
and the great centaur said: "These are tyrants
who dealt in blood and pillaged.

Here they cry for their pitiless crimes;
here's Alexander, and fierce Dionysius
who gave Sicily painful years.

And that forehead with such black hair
is Azzolino; and that other blond one
is Opizzo d'Esti, who really

was killed by his stepson up there in the world."
Then I turned to the poet, and he said:
"Now he is first to you, and I second."

A little further on the centaur stopped
over people who, down to the neck,
seemed to be coming out of the boiling.

He showed us a shadow to one side, alone,
saying: "This one split in two God's
heart that still bleeds on the Thames."

Then I saw people out of the river
as far as their heads and trunks;
I knew plenty of these.

More and more
the blood lowered, until it only cooked their feet;
and then we could pass.

"As you see here
the boiling that lessens,"
said the centaur, "I want you to believe

that over there more and more down
the bottom falls, until it reaches
where tyranny must wail.

Divine justice strikes
Attila, who was a scourge on earth,
and Pirrhys and Sextus, and eternally milks

their tears, let loose by boiling,
from Rinier of Corneto to Rinier the Madman,
who made the streets a war zone."
Then he turned and went back across the ford.

Canto XIII

Nessus had not yet arrived there
when we made our way into a woods
not marked by any path.

No green leaves, but a dark color;
no straight branches, but knobby and twisted;
no apples, but thorns with poison.

No harsher are the woods
for savage creatures that hate has cultivated
between Cecina and Corneto.

There the ugly Harpies nest
who drove out the Strophades and Trojans
with a sad announcement of future harm.

They have wide wings, human necks and faces,
feet with claws, a huge feathered belly;
they wail high in their strange trees.

And my good teacher: "Before you go in any further,
know you're in the second turning,"
he stated, telling me, "and you will be

until you come to the horrible sands.
But look carefully and you'll see
things that will make you doubt what I say."

I heard from all sides wailing
and saw no one who could have done it;
so I, confused, stopped.

I think he thought I thought
that so many voices came from among these branches
from people hiding from us.

But the teacher said, "If you snap
a twig from one of these plants,
so will your thoughts be cut short."

So I stretched out a hand a little ahead
and pulled a little branch from a thorn bush;
and its trunk shrieked: "Why do you break me?"

It ran with brown blood
and said again: "Why do you tear me?
Have you no spirit of pity?

We were men now made bushes;
your hand would have had more pity
if we had been serpents' souls."

As a green stick burning
at one end, that at the other hisses
and drips as wind leaves it,

so from the broken splinter came together
words and blood; and I let the end
fall and stood like a man in fear.

"If he could have believed before,"
responded my wise man, "wounded soul,
what he'd seen in my rhymes,

he wouldn't have stretched out his hand against you,
but the incredible thing made me
push him to this act, and it burdens me.

But tell him, if you can, if there is instead
some way he can make it up to you, refreshing your fame
in the world above, where he's allowed to return."

And the trunk: "If your sweet speech attracts me,
so that I can't be quiet, don't take offense
if I am invested in speaking a little.

I am he who had both keys
to Federigo's heart, and who turned them,
locking and unlocking, so smoothly,

I kept from every man his secrets;
I was so faithful to that glorious job
that I lost sleep and life.

The deserving one who never
took her whoring eyes off Caesar's home,
common death and the sin of courts

inflamed all minds against me;
and the inflamed so inflamed Augustus,
that glad honors turned to sad fights.

My mind disdainfully
believing that to die would be to escape disdain,
unjustly set me against my own justice.

By the new roots of this wood,

I swear to you I never broke faith
with my lord, so deserving of honor.

And if one of you goes back to the world,
comfort my memory, that lies
under the blow envy gave it."

Silence a while, and then, "Given that he's quiet,"
said the poet to me, "don't lose time,
but speak, and ask him if you want more."

Then I to him: "Ask him again
what you think will satisfy me;
I can't, so much pity runs through me."

So he started again: "If this man does for you
freely what you ask of him,
imprisoned spirit, be pleased again

to tell us how the soul is tied
in these knots; and tell us, if you can,
if you're ever freed from these limbs."

The trunk sighed strongly, and then
that wind changed into a voice:
"My answer to you will be brief.

When the ferocious soul leaves
the body it's torn itself from,
Minos sends it to the seventh pit.

It falls in the woods, in a place it didn't choose,
wherever fortune sweeps it,

there germinating.

It grows into a sapling and a forest tree;
the Harpies, feeding on its leaves,
hurt it, and for the pain an opening.

Like others, we will come to claim what we have shed,
but not like the others will we put it on again;
it wouldn't be fair if we put back on what we stripped off.

We'll drag them here, and
all our bodies will hang in the forest,
each from a thorn of his molested shadow."

We were still paying attention to the trunk,
believing it would want to say something else,
when we were surprised by a noise,

like a man who
senses the pig and the hunt at his post,
hears the beast and branches crashing.

And then two on the left,
naked and scratched, fleeing so hard
they broke through every thicket.

The one in front: "Run help, run help, death!"
And the other, taking too long,
shouted, "Lano,

your legs weren't so fast at the Toppo games!"
And then, maybe because he was out of breath,
tried to hide in a bush.

Behind them the jungle was full
of black bitches, starving and fast
as greyhounds off the chain.

They got their teeth into the one who knelt,
and tore him limb from limb;
then carried off those painful members.

My escort took me by the hand,
led me to the bush that wept
in vain for its bleeding wounds.

"Jacob," he said, "of Sant'Andrea,
why did you use me to cover you?
How is your underhanded life my fault?"

When the teacher stopped over it,
he said, "Who were you, who because of all these stabs
still blow out blood with your sad sermon?"

And he to us: "Oh, souls who arrived
to see the dishonest killing
that stripped from me my leaves,

gather them at the foot of this sad trunk.
I was from the city that changed John the Baptist
for the God of War as its first leader; and because of this,

his art will always make it miserable;
if it weren't that, at the Arno pass,
some view of his remains,

those citizens who rebuilt
on the ashes Attila left
would have worked for nothing;
I made my noose out of my homes."

Canto XIV

Because the charity of my native land
pushed me, I gathered the scattered leaves
and gave them to him, who was already faint.

Then we came to where
the second turn parted from the third, and where
we saw justice's horrible work.

To explain the new things well,
I'd say we arrived at a flat land
that removes every plant from its bed.

The painful forest was a necklace
around it, like the moat of sorrow is;
here we stopped at the very edge.

The arena was of arid, deep sand,
not different from that
under Cato's feet.

Vengeance of God, how you
should be feared by each person who reads
what I saw before my eyes!

Many herds of naked souls,
all crying miserably,
who appeared to be punished by different laws.

Some lay on the ground,
some sat huddled,
and others wandered continually.

Most wandered around,
and fewer lay in torment,
though their tongues wailed most.

Over all the sand, slowly
rained dilated flakes of fire,
like snow in mountains without wind.

As Alexander, in the hot lands
of India, saw
flames fall on his troops and on the ground

commanded they trample the soil
so the vapor
was extinguished,

eternal flames fell
and the sand caught fire as if
under flint, and doubled the pain.

Restlessly danced
miserable hands, here and there
slapping off fresh sparks.

I began: "Teacher, you who defeat
all things, except those hard demons
who came out against us at the gate,

who is that important one who doesn't seem to care
about the flames and lies scornful
as if the rain doesn't hurt him?"

And he himself, who seemed to realize
I asked my boss about him,
shouted: "What I was alive, so I am dead.

May Jove wear out his factory where he
forged the bright thunderbolt
that struck me my last day!

If he wore out all the others one by one
at Mongibello's black forge
calling, 'Good Vulcan, help, help!'

as he did at the fight of Phlegra,
and shot at me with all his might,
he would not enjoy his revenge."

Then my boss spoke with such force
that I hadn't heard him so loud:
"Capaneus, as

your arrogance never gets less, you suffer more;
in no suffering except your rage
would your fury double your pain."

Then he turned back to me with a better tone
saying: "He was one of the seven kings
at the siege of Thebes; and had—and appears to have—

disdain of God, and doesn't seem to pray to him much;
but as I told him, his disrespect
pretty well decorates his chest.

Now come behind me and watch out that you don't put

your feet on the burning sand
but always in the woods."

Quietly we came to where
a little stream spurts out of the forest
whose redness still terrifies me.

As from the river Bulicame flows a brook
the sinful women share,
so this one ran down the sand.

Its bottom and both sides
were made of stone, and the edge of its banks;
I realized that the passage was over there.

"Among all the things I've shown you,
since we came through the gate
whose entry is denied to no one,

your eyes have discovered nothing
as notable as this present river
that kills the flames above it."

These words out of my boss;
so I begged him for the great meal
he'd made me desire.

"In mid-sea sits a wasteland,"
he said then, "called Crete,
under whose king the world was chaste.

There was a cheerful mountain
with water and leaves, called Ida,

86

now deserted like something laid waste.

Rhea chose it to faithfully cradle
her son, and to hide him
when he cried, had people shout.

A great ancient man stands straight in the mountain;
his shoulders turned toward Dammiata,
he looks at Rome as if it were his mirror.

His head is shaped of fine gold,
and his arms and chest of pure silver,
then he's brass to the balls;

from there down he's the best grade of iron,
except the right foot of baked clay;
and he stands more on that than on the other, erect.

Each part of him, except the gold, is broken
by a crack that drips tears
that, running, carve out this cavern.

Coursing rock to rock through this valley,
they make Acheron, Styx and Phlegethon, the Rivers of
Woe, Hatred and Fire,
then going down this narrow shower

end there, where there is no more descent,
making Cocytus, the Lake of Lamentation; and what kind
of pool,
you will see, but here I say nothing."

And I to him: "If the present stream

begins like this in our world,
why does it appear only at this end?"

And he to me: "You know the place is round,
and you have come through a lot,
always on the left, down to the bottom,

but you still haven't turned the full circle;
so, if something new appears,
your face doesn't have to look so amazed!"

And I again: "Teacher, where are
the Phlegethon, River of Fire, and the Lethe, Oblivion?
About one you're silent,
and the other is made of this rain."

"All your questions please me,"
he responded, "but the red and boiling water
might as well have answered one of them.

You'll see the Lethe, the River of Oblivion, but out of this
moat,
there where the souls bathe
once their guilty penance is removed."

Then he said: "Now it's time to leave
the woods; stay behind me:
the edges that make the path aren't burning,
and all the sparks above them are put out."

Canto XV

Now we go along one of the hard margins;
and the brook's steam mists above,
and saves the water and the walls from the fires.

Like the Flemish between Cadsand and Bruges,
afraid of the flood hurtling toward them,
build a wall so the sea will flee,

and those Paduans along the Brenta,
to defend their towns and castles
before Carentana feels the heat,

like those images these were made,
not so high or thick;
whoever he was, a master made them.

Now we were so far from the forest
that I couldn't have seen where it was
if I'd turned back,

when we met a squadron of souls
who came along the bank, and each
looked at us like night watchmen

look at each other under a new moon;
and they frowned at us
like an old tailor at the eye of a needle.

So eyeballed by such a family,
one of them knew me and caught me
by the hem and shouted, "What a marvel!"

and I, when he stretched out his arm to me,
I fixed my eyes on his cooked aspect
so that his scorched face could not prevent

my intellect's recognizing him;
and bending my hand to his face,
I responded: "Are you here, Ser Brunetto?"

And he: "Son, don't be displeased
if Brunetto Latino turns back with you a little
and lets them trail on."

I said to him: "As much as I can, I beg you,
and if you would like, I will sit with you,
if it's all right with the man I'm following."

"Oh son," he said, "any of this gang
who stop at all must lie down for a hundred years
without fanning themselves when the fire alights.

But go on. I'll follow your robe
and then rejoin my band
that goes crying about their eternal wrongs."

I didn't dare get down from the street
to go on his level; but with head bowed,
I was like a man who walks reverently.

He began: "What fortune of destiny
brought you here before your last day?
And who's this gentleman showing you the way?"

"Up there, in the serene life,"
I responded to him, "I got lost in a valley,
before my age was full.

But yesterday morning I turned my back on it;
this man appeared to me as I turned back
and leads me back home by this road."

And he to me: "If you follow your star,
you can't fail to sail to a glorious port,
if I understood well in the beautiful life.

And if I hadn't died so soon,
seeing Heaven so kind to you,
I would have comforted you in your work.

But that ungrateful, evil people
who came down from Fiesole ages ago,
a bunch of backwoods hillbillies,

will become, for your own good, your enemy,
as is right; among bitter berries
sweet figs don't bear fruit.

Old fame in the world calls them blind,
a greedy, envious, stuck-up people:
wash off the taint of their customs.

Your fate reserves a lot of honor for you;
one party and another will be hungry
for you, but the grass will grow far from the goat.

Let the beasts of Fiesole chew on

themselves and not touch the plant,
if any still grows on their pile of shit,

where the holy seed is coming back to life
of those Romans who remained here after
it became the nest of so much malice."

"If my request were fulfilled,"
I responded to him, "you would not yet be
banished from human nature;

fixed in my mind and heart is
the dear good fatherly image
of you, when, from time to time,

you taught me how a man becomes eternal;
and how grateful I am, while I live,
must be made clear in my language.

What you narrate of my course I write,
and keep it to share, with another text,
with a lady who will understand, if I can get to her.

This much I want to show you,
if my conscience doesn't bother me:
that I am ready for Fortune to do as it wants.

Such news isn't new to my ears:
but Fortune turns its wheel
as it likes, and the farmer his shovel."

My teacher then
turned his right cheek back and looked at me;

then he said: "To listen well is to take note."

Speaking none the less I go
with Ser Brunetto, and I ask who are
his most noteworthy and highly placed companions.

And he to me: "To know some of them is good;
of others it would be praiseworthy to be silent,
since time would be short for so much noise.

To sum it up, know that all were religious men
and great writers of great fame,
stained in the world with the same sin.

Priscian goes with that wretched gang,
and Francesco d'Accorso, also; and you'd
have seen, if you cared for such punks,

the one who the servant of servants
transferred from the Arno to Bacchiglione,
where he left his sin-distended nerves.

I would say more; but coming along and speaking
can't go on any longer; for I see
there new smoke rising from the sand.

People are coming that I can't be with.
I commend my *Treasure* to you,
where I live on, and ask for nothing more."

Then he turned back and seemed like those
who run at Verona for the green ribbon
across the countryside; and he seemed like those

who win, not the one who loses.

Canto XVI

I was already at the place where
the water roared, falling in the next circle,
like the rumble of bees,

when three shadows left
running from a group passing
under the rain of bitter martyrdom.

They came near us, and each shouted:
"Hold up! you whose clothes
seem to be from our depraved land."

Oh, what wounds I saw on their arms and legs,
new and old, burned on by the flames!
It still hurts me when I remember them.

My professor listened to their cry,
turned his face toward me, and "Now wait;"
he said, "one wants to be courteous to these men.

If falling fire weren't
the nature of the place, I'd say
haste would be better for you than them."

When we stopped, they started again
their old verse; and when they reached us,
the three of them made a wheel.

As champion wrestlers naked and greased
look for a hold and an advantage
before they trade off parries and points,

so wheeling, each face
directed at me, so that their necks strained back
as their feet traveled forward.

And "If the misery of this sandy place
makes you disrespect us and our prayers,"
started one, "and our darkened, boiled faces,

may our fame move your mind
to tell us who you are, on living feet
so safely brought through Hell.

This man whose footsteps you see me walk in,
all nude and hairless as he goes,
was of a greater rank than you would believe;

grandson of the good Gualdrada;
War Guide was his name, and in his life
he made do with good sense and a sword.

The other, scrunching sand beside me,
is Tegghiaio Aldobrandi, who
should have been listened to in the world above.

And I, put with them on this cross,
was Jacob Rusticucci, and certainly
my fierce wife, more than anyone else, destroys me."

If I'd been shielded from the fire,
I would have thrown myself down there among them,
and my professor would have suffered it to happen,

but since I would have burned and baked,
fear defeated the good will
that made me greedy to hug them.

Then I started: "Not disrespect but despair
fixed your condition so deeply inside me
that it will take a long time to free myself of it,

as soon as my teacher said to me
words that made me think
people like you were coming.

I'm from your land, and always
your work and your honored names
were affectionately retraced and heard.

I leave the gall and go for sweet fruits
promised by my honest leader;
but I have to get to the center before I can get them."

"May your soul for a long time carry
your body," he responded again,
"and may your fame shine after you pass;

tell us if courtesy and bravery remain
in our city as once upon a time,
or if they've both been thrown out;

because William Borsiere, grieving
with us for a little while now, over there with those guys,
crucifies us with what he says."

"The new people and their quick profits

have generated such arrogance and excess,
Florence, in you, so that you already grieve."

This I cried with my face lifted;
and the three, who took that as answer,
looked at each other as at the truth.

"If at other times it costs you so little,"
they all responded, "to satisfy another,
you must be glad you can talk when you want to.

So, if you get out of these dark places
and go back to see the beautiful stars again,
when you'll be happy to say, 'I was there,'

tell people our stories."
Then they broke the wheel, and fled
as if their legs were wings.

An amen can't be said
as fast as they disappeared;
it seemed to my teacher time to go.

I followed him, and we hadn't gone far
when the sound of water was so close
that we could hardly hear ourselves talk.

Like that river that
rises from Vision Mountain
on the left coast of the Apennines,

called Still Water up there before
it tumbles down into its low bed,

and at Forli loses that name,

rumbling over San Benedetto
of the Alps to fall in one cascade
like a thousand,

so, down a sheer cliff,
we found dark water thundering
so that it would have damaged our ears.

I had a rope around my waist
I'd planned
to catch the painted leopard with.

After I untied it,
as my boss told me to,
I gave it to him gathered up and twisted.

He turned to the right,
and far out from the edge,
flung it into the abyss.

 "Surely something unusual has to answer,"
I said to myself, "that weird signal
my teacher follows with his eyes."

How cautious men should be
when they're near those who don't see actions only,
but through their sensitivity look into thoughts!

He said to me: "Soon we'll see rise
what I'm waiting for; and what your mind can only dream
of

must soon be uncovered to your eyes."

Always, when truth has the face of a lie,
a man should sooner shut his mouth
than, blameless, still be shamed;

but I can't be silent here; and by the verses
of this *Comedy*, reader, I swear to you
—may it not be banned for long—

I saw through that dark thick air
come swimming up a figure
incredible to any strong heart,

like one who goes down
to loosen a caught anchor
or something trapped in the sea,
reaching up and pulling in his feet.

Canto XVII

"Here is the beast with the arrow tail,
who crossed the mountains and breaks down walls and
weapons!
Here he is who defiles the world!"

My boss started talking like this to me
and made a sign to it to come to shore
near the end of the rocky walkway.

And that filthy image of fraud
approached, its head and chest on the bank
but not its tail.

Its face was of an honest man,
kindness skin-deep,
and all the rest was serpent;

two paws hairy to the armpits;
the back and chest and both sides
painted with dots and circles.

More colorful background and decoration
were never woven into Tartar and Turkish cloth,
nor were such patterns weaved by Arachne.

As boats come sometimes to the shore,
part in water and part on land,
and as there between the beer-drinking Germans

the beaver sets up to make its war,
so that vilest beast settled

on the stone border that sealed off the sand.

Its tail writhed in the nothingness,
twisting up the venomous fork
that armed the point, like a scorpion.

The boss said: "Now we must
turn our way a little to get to that
foul beast laid out there."

So we went down to the right,
ten steps along the edge,
keeping away from the sand and flames.

And when we came even with it,
a little further off I saw on the sand
people seated at the sheer drop.

Then the teacher: "So that complete
experience of this circle can go with you,"
he said to me, "go, and see how they are.

Keep your talk short;
until you come back, I'll talk with this,
so he'll concede to us his strong shoulders."

So still higher, to the extreme top
of that seventh circle, all alone,
I went where the sad people sat.

Their mourning poured out of their eyes
from here, from there; their hands tried to protect them
now from the flames, now from the hot sand,

not unlike dogs in summer
with muzzle or foot when bitten
by fleas or by flies.

I eyed certain faces
that the painful fire fell on
but knew none; but I realized

that from each one's neck hung a pouch
that had a certain color and certain symbol,
and there their eyes fed.

And as I came among them staring,
on a yellow purse I saw the blue
of a lion's face and countenance.

Then, letting my gaze run its course,
I saw another like red blood
showing a goose whiter than butter.

And one with a fat blue pregnant pig
as the symbol on his white sack
said to me: "What are you doing in this pit?

Now get out of here; and since you're still alive,
know that my neighbor Vitaliano
will soon sit here on my left side.

Among these Florentines, I am Paduan;
often they thunder on my ears
shouting: 'Come, the knight king

who will wear the pouch with three goats!'"
Here he distorted his mouth and stuck out
his tongue, like an ox that licks its nose.

And I, fearing that to stay longer would irritate
him who had just admonished me to stay a little while,
turned myself back from the weary souls.

I found my boss had climbed up
on the fierce demon's back,
and he said to me: "Now be strong and determined.

We'll go down these so-called stairs;
you ride up front because I want to be in the middle
so his tail can't do any harm."

As a man taken by shivering
whose fingernails have already died
trembles at the sight of shade,

so I became at the import of these words;
but shame menaced me
that, in front of my good sir, I should try to be a strong
servant.

I climbed up and sat on those enormous shoulders;
I wanted to say, but my voice wouldn't come
as I expected: "Make sure you hold onto me."

But he, who had helped me overcome
at other times, as soon as I mounted,
grabbed me and supported me with his arms

and said: "Geryon, now move:
wide circles, and go down slowly;
think of the new added weight you have."

Like a boat leaving the place,
back and back he pulls himself,
and then, feeling himself floating,

revolved his tail to where his chest was,
stretched it, like an eel, moved,
and with his paws gathered to himself the air.

Greater fear, I don't think,
Phaeton felt when he abandoned the reins
and the sky burned, as we see it now;

nor when miserable Icarus
felt his feathers plucked out by the melting wax
as his father shouted to him, "You're going the wrong
way!"

than mine, when I saw
air everywhere and saw
nothing but the demon.

On it goes, swimming slowly, slowly;
round it goes down, but I'm aware of nothing
but, at my face and from beneath me, wind.

I heard already at my right hand the whirlpool
under us make a horrible splashing,
so I looked down.

Then I feared the abyss
when I saw fires and heard screams;
and I held on tighter, trembling.

And then I saw what I hadn't seen before,
going down and turning, the great terrors
drawing nearer on every side.

Like a falcon that's been a long time on the wing,
and not seeing a lure or bird
makes the falconer say, "Hey, come down!"

he descends tiredly,
by a hundred turns, and far away
from its master alights, disdainful and pouting,

so Geryon put us at the bottom,
at the very foot of the jagged rock,
and, unburdened of our bodies,
shot off like an arrow from a string.

Canto XVIII

There is a place in Hell called Evil Trenches,
all of iron-colored stone
like the circle that runs around it.

Right in the middle of the malignant countryside
yawns a well very wide and deep
whose place I will explain.

The belt is round
between the well and the foot of a high, hard bank,
and its bottom is ten distant valleys.

As where, to guard the walls,
more and more moats belt the castles,
their placing

made such an image as this;
and as such fortresses, from their gates
to the farthest bank, are bridges,

so from the edge of the broken rock
jutted down banks and pits
to the well that stops and gathers them.

In this place, shaken off the back
of Geryon, we found ourselves; and the poet
took off to the left, and I moved after him.

At my right hand I saw new anguish,
new torments, and new whip-masters
that filled the first ditch.

In its bottom, the sinners were naked;
in the middle they came toward us, turning;
further over, with us, but taking larger steps,

like Romans with the huge crowds
the year of Jubilee, upon the bridge
had to pass the people through somehow,

so on one side everyone faces forward
toward the castle and goes to St. Peter's,
and on the other they go toward the mountain.

Here and there on the dark rock
I saw horned demons with great whips
who struck them cruelly from behind.

Oh, how they made them lift their heels
with the first strikes! None
waited for a second or third.

While I walked, my eyes were
caught by one of them; and I suddenly said:
"I've already had my fill of the sight of this one."

I stopped in my tracks to figure him out;
and the sweet guide stayed with me
and agreed to let me turn back a few steps.

And that whipped one thought he hid
by lowering his face; it did him little good,
for I said: "You, looking down at the ground,

if your features aren't false,
you're Venedico Enemy-Hunter.
But what put you in this pungent sauce?"

And he to me: "Against my will I'll tell you;
but I am forced by your clear speech,
that makes me remember the old world.

It was I who brought Ghiso the Beautiful
to do the will of the Marquis,
despite how the story is told.

I am not the only lamenting Bolognese;
this place is full of them,
though not so many tongues have learned

to say 'yep' like a Bolognese between Sàvena and Reno,
and if you want more good faith or testimony,
bring to mind our heartfelt greed."

So speaking, a demon struck him
with his whip and said, "Get away,
pimp! There are no women to do a trick here."

I went back to my escort;
in a few steps we came to
where a ledge came out of the cliff.

We went up this easily enough
and turned to the right upon its ridge
and left those eternal circles.

When we were there where the hollow

underneath makes a passage for whipped souls,
the guide said: "Hold up; let

these born sinners get a look at you,
whose faces you haven't seen yet
but who have been coming along with us."

From the old bridge we looked at the line
that came toward us from the other side,
similarly whipped.

And the good teacher, without my asking,
said to me, "Look at the great one who comes
and doesn't spare a tear for his pain:

what a regal aspect he still has!
He's Jason, who with heart and cleverness
deprived the Colchis of the Golden Fleece.

He passed by the island of Lemnos
after the ardent, pitiless women
had put all their men to death.

There, with signs and ornate words
he deceived Hypsipyle, the young woman
who first deceived all the other women.

He left her there, pregnant, alone;
such guilt condemns him to such suffering;
and this is also Medea's revenge.

With him go those who deceive;
that's enough of the first valley

to know, and of those in its jaws."

We were already where the narrow street
crosses the second ridge
and makes of that another arching shoulder.

Then we heard people who whined
in the next ravine, and with their muzzles snorted,
and slapped themselves with their open palms.

The banks were slimed with mold
breathed out from down below that crusts there,
assaulting eyes and nose.

The bottom is so deep that there is no
place to see it from without mounting
the arch's back, where the ridge is highest.

There we came; and there in the pit
I saw people stuffed in a latrine
that seemed to flow from human sewage.

While I searched down there with my eye
I saw a head so heavy with shit
that he didn't appear to be priest or parishioner.

He shouted at me: "Why are you so greedy
to look at me more than the other ugly ones?"
And I to him: "Because, if I remember well,

I've seen you already with dry hair,
and you are Alessio Interminei of Lucca:
that's why I eye you more than all the others."

And he then, beating his pumpkin head:
"Down here I'm drowning in the bullshit
that never glued my tongue."

Then apprised the guide: "Stick out,"
he said, "your head a little more forward,
so that your eyes can make out the face

of that filthy slovenly slut
down there scratching herself with fingernails full of shit,
squatting and standing.

She is Taide, the whore who responded
to her dude when he said 'Have I pleased
you enormously?': 'Even marvelously!'
And with that may our sight be satiated."

Canto XIX

Oh Simon Magus, oh miserable followers
who misuse the things of God that
should be the brides of his bounty, and immorally

prostitute them for gold and silver,
now the trumpet must sound for you
because you stay in the third ravine.

We were already at the following tomb,
mounted to the cliff
where the point was straight above the middle of the pit.

Oh, summit of knowledge, how great is the art
you show in Heaven, in earth and in the evil world,
and how great the justice your virtue gives out!

I saw on the sides and bottom
the livid stone full of holes,
all large and each round.

They didn't seem to me less wide nor bigger
than those in my beautiful St. John,
made for the place of the baptizers;

one of them, not many years ago,
I broke for someone drowning inside;
and may this be my pledge that sets straight every man.

From the mouth of each rose out
the feet and legs of a sinner
to the thighs, and the rest was stuck.

The bottoms of their feet were both on fire;
their joints jerked so strongly
they would have snapped restraints and ties.

As flames on oily things
move on the extremities,
so did these from the heels to the toes.

"Who is that one, teacher, who in his agony
jerks around more than the rest of his gang,"
I said, "and redder flames suck?"

And he to me: "If you want I'll take you
down by the lowest bank,
and you'll know from him about himself and his
mistakes."

And I: "Whatever pleases you is beautiful to me:
you're the boss, and you know that I won't go against
what you want, and you know what isn't said."

Then we came to the fourth wall;
we turned and descended on the left hand
down to the bottom stabbed with holes and narrow.

The good teacher didn't put me down from his side
until I reached the broken pit
of one who cried with his kicks.

"Whoever you are upside-down,
sad soul stuck like a post,"
I started to say, "if you can, say something."

114

I stood like a friar who confesses
the sneaky assassin who, when he is absolved,
calls him back to stop death.

And he shouted: "Are you already standing there?
Are you already standing there, Boniface?
The writings lied to me by several years!

Have you already had enough
of what you weren't afraid to take and trick
the beautiful Lady out of, and then do her wrong?"

I was like those who stand,
not understanding the response they've gotten,
not sure if they're mocked, and not knowing how to
respond.

Then Virgil said: "Tell him right away:
'I'm not him; I'm not the one you believe'";
and I answered as he told me to do.

So the spirit waved his feet;
then, sighing and with a complaining voice,
he said to me: "So what are you asking of me?

If finding out who I am means so much to you
that you crossed the bank,
know that I was dressed in the mantle of greatness;

and I was truly the son of the mother bear Orsini,
so greedy to advance the Orsini little bears,
that, up there, possessions, and down here, myself, I put

in my pocket.

Under my head are the others
who went ahead of me, selling sacred things,
flattened in the fissures in the rock.

I will fall down there too when
the man I thought you were gets here,
when I asked you abruptly.

But I've already spent more time with my feet cooking
upside down
than he will spend planted with red feet:

after him will come, with uglier works,
from the west, a lawless pastor,
fit to cover him and me.

He will be a new Jason, whom we read about
in Maccabees; and as the king was soft on him,
so will be the king of France."

I don't know if I was too crazy,
but I answered him in this way:
"Hey, now tell me: how much treasure

did our lord first want from St. Peter
before he would put the keys into his keeping?
Certainly he didn't ask anything but, 'Follow me.'

Neither Peter nor the others took Matthias's
gold or silver, when he was chosen
for the place lost by the guilty soul.

So stay there, for you are well punished;
and keep an eye on the evilly gotten money
that made you get so tough with King Charles.

And if I were not still held back
by reverence for the highest keys
you held in the happy life,

I would use words still more grave;
your greed saddens the world,
walking all over the good and uplifting the depraved.

The Evangelist was thinking of pastors like you
when the one who sits upon the waters
he saw whoring with kings;

she who was born with seven heads
and gets her fight from the ten horns,
as long as virtue pleased her husband.

You have made yourselves a god of gold and silver;
and how are you different from those who worship idols,
except that they pray to one, and you to a hundred?

Oh, Constantine, how much evil you mothered,
not by your conversion, but that dowry
your first rich father took from you!"

And while I sang such tunes to him,
and anger or conscience bit him,
he kicked out with both feet.

I think it pleased my guide well,
with such a pleasant contented set of his mouth he listened
to the sound of the true words I expressed.

Because with both arms he grabbed me;
and then with me all on his chest,
he went back up the way he had come down.

Nor did he tire of holding me so close
but carried me to the top of the arch
that curves from the fourth to the fifth wall.

Here softly he put down his burden,
gently on the broken steep cliff
that would be a hard path for a mountain goat.
From there I discovered another valley.

Canto XX

I have to make verses about new pain
and give substance to the twentieth canto
of the first song, which is about those submerged.

By now I was all ready
to look into the depths uncovered,
bathed in the anguish of weeping;

and I saw people in the curved valley
coming, quietly and with tears streaming, at the pace
of litany-singers in this world.

I looked down them,
and incredibly they appeared to be twisted,
each one, from chin to chest,

with their heads turned on their shoulders,
walking backwards as they came on
because they couldn't see ahead.

Perhaps palsy
twists someone all up that way;
but I have seen nothing like it and don't think it possible.

If God lets you, reader, take the fruit
of your lesson, think for yourself
how I might keep my face dry

when our image, up close,
I saw so contorted that the tears from their eyes
ran into their butt cracks.

Certainly I cried, leaning on a rock
of the hard cliff, so that my escort
said to me: "Still as stupid as the rest?

Here piety lives when pity has died;
who is more degenerate than someone
who thinks that divine judgment is passionate?

Put your head up, up, and see him who
split the earth open under the Thebans' eyes;
so that they all shouted, 'Where are you running,

Amphiaraus? Why are you leaving the war?'
And he didn't stop ruining the valley
until he reached Minos, who seizes everyone.

Look how his chest has been made of his shoulders;
because he turned to see too much ahead,
he looks back and makes a backward way.

See Tiresias, who mutated
from male to female,
changing all his members;

and first, later, he had to beat apart
the two entwined serpents with his wand,
before he got back his masculine feathers.

Aruns's back is to the other's belly,
who, in the Luni hills, where
the Carrarese plow who live below,

between white marble, made a cave
his dwelling, where he could look at the stars
and the sea unobstructed.

And that woman who covers her breasts,
which you don't see, with her hair down,
who has on that side all the hairy skin,

was Manto, who searched many lands,
then put herself there where I was born;
here I'd like you to listen to me a little.

After her father left this life,
and the city of Bacchus was enslaved,
she wandered the world for a long time.

High in beautiful Italy lies a lake
at the foot of the Alps that shuts Germany
in over Tyrol, named Benaco.

A thousand springs, I believe, and more bathe
Garda to Val Camonica and Pennino
with water that stagnates in the lake.

There is a place in the middle where the pastors
of Trent, Brescia and Verona
would make the sign of the cross, if they passed that way.

Peschiera sits, beautiful and strong fortress
confronting the Brescians and Bergamans,
where the bank around descends lowest.

Here must fall all the water

that can't stay in Benaco's bosom,
making a river down through green pastures.

As soon as the water runs,
it is no longer Benaco but called Mencio
all the way to Governo, where it falls into the Po.

It hasn't run far before it finds a plain
where it spreads into a swamp;
and the soil in summer is poor.

So, passing that way, the solitary virgin
saw earth in the middle of a marsh,
uncultivated and naked of inhabitants.

There, to get away from people,
she stayed with her servants to practice her magic,
and lived, and left her empty body.

Then the scattered men
converged on that place, a stronghold
because of the swamp all around.

They made a city over those dead bones;
and for she who had first chosen that place,
called it Mantua without other magic.

There were a lot more inhabitants
before the madness of Casalodi
was fooled by Pinamonte.

If you ever hear
of the origin of my land described another way,

don't let a lie pass for the truth."

And I: "Teacher, your reasoning
sounds so certain, and so wins my faith,
that others would be dead coals to me.

But tell me, of the people going by,
do you see anyone noteworthy?
That's all my mind keeps going back to."

Then he said to me: "That one
with the beard from his throat to his brown shoulders
was—when Greece was emptied of men

so there hardly remained one in a cradle—a
fortuneteller, who gave advice to Calchas
at Aulis, when to cut the navy's first tether.

Eurypylus was his name, and so sings
my high tragedy in some place:
you know it well who know it all.

The other whose haunches are so little
was Michael Scott, who really
knew the game of magical fraud.

See Guido Bonatti; see Asdente,
who now would like his leather and his thread
but repents too late.

See the sad women who gave up needle,
spool and spinning and made themselves diviners,
making black magic with herbs and images.

But now, come; already Cain-in-the-moon confines
both hemispheres and touches the ocean waves
under Seville with his thorns;

and already last night the moon was round;
remember well, it didn't hurt you
at any time in the deep forest."
He spoke like this to me as we walked.

Canto XXI

So from bridge to bridge, speaking
of things my comedy does not care to sing about,
we came to the highest point when

we stopped to see the next fissure
of the Evil Trenches and the other useless crying;
and I saw incredible darkness.

As the Venetian arsenal
boils sticky pitch
to cover leaky wood

because their ships cannot sail—and instead
one makes a new ship and one stops up
the leaks on his that has made more voyages;

one hammers the prow and one the stern;
others make oars and others twist rope;
one mends the mainsail and others mend the rigging—

in this way, not by fire but by divine art,
boiled down there a thick tar
that glued the banks everywhere.

I saw the tar but saw nothing in it
but the bubbles the boiling raised
all swell and resettle, compressed.

While I looked down there, fixated,
my leader, saying "Look out, look out!"
pulled me to him from where I stood.

Then I turned like a man anxious
to see what he must flee
and whose fear suddenly tears him apart,

whose looking doesn't stop his getting out of there:
and I saw behind us a black devil
running up the ridge, coming on.

Oh, how feral his aspect!
And his movements vicious,
with his wings opened over his light feet!

His shoulder, pointed and high,
carried a sinner's two hips,
and he held him by the sinews of his heels.

From our bridge he said: "Hey, Evil Claws,
here's one of the good old boys of Santa Zita!
Throw him under, and I'll go back for another

from that land, which is well supplied with them.
Every man there sells public offices—except Bonturo;
from no, for money, they can make you a *yes*!"

He threw him down, and up the hard cliff
he turned; and never was a mastiff freed
so fast to go after a burglar.

That one sank and came up again turned over;
but the demons covered by the bridge
shouted: "Here is no place for the Holy Face!

126

Here you don't swim like in the Serchio!
So, if you don't want any of our claws,
don't come out over the tar."

Then they pierced him with more than a hundred hooks,
saying: "You have to dance under cover here
 and, if you can, hide your stealing,"

as chefs make their assistants
stuff down in the middle of the cauldron
the meat with the skewers, so it won't float.

The good teacher: "So they won't guess
you're here," he said to me, "squat down
behind a cliff, so you have a screen;

and for any offense against me,
don't you be afraid; I've taken account of things,
and, the last time, I had a skirmish like this."

When he passed the head of the bridge
and reached the sixth bank,
 he had to put on a brave front.

With all that fury and that storm
like dogs on a poor man's back
who suddenly stops to beg,

they came out from under the bridge
and turned all their grappling hooks on him;
but he shouted: "No one of you had better commit that
crime!

Before one of your hooks strikes me,
send out one of you to listen to me,
and then take counsel together about using your hooks on
me."

All shouted: "Evil Tail should go!"
So one moved—and the others stayed where they were—
and he came to him saying: "What good will this do
him?"

"Do you believe, Evil Tail, that you could see me
here," said my teacher,
"safe despite all your schemes,

without divine will and fated destiny?
Let us go, because it's wanted in Heaven
that I show someone this savage road."

Then his pride fell so
that he dropped his hook to his feet,
and he said to the others: "All right now; don't hurt him."

And my leader said to me: "Hey, you, squatting
in the rocks of the bridge,
now it's safe to join me again."

So I moved and hurried over to him;
and the devils all came forward,
so that I was afraid they wouldn't keep the pact,

just like I'd seen the infantry
given safe passage out of Caprona,
seeing themselves among so many enemies.

I put my whole body
up against my leader, and I didn't take my eyes
off their faces, which weren't nice.

They bent down their hooks and "Want me to touch him,"
said one to another, "in his butt?"
And they responded: "Yes, let him have it."

But that demon who was talking
with my leader, turned all of a sudden
and said: "Put it down, put it down, Rumple!"

Then he said to us: "You can't go further
along this cliff because
the sixth arch is shattered into pieces at the bottom.

If you'd like to go ahead,
go down this rock;
close by is another cliff that makes a path.

Yesterday, in five hours, it was
one thousand two hundred sixty-six
years that the path was broken.

I'm sending some of my guys
that way to look for anyone out for some fresh air;
go with them because they won't bully you.

Step forward, Bent Wing and Frost-stomper,"
he began to say, "and you, Dirty Dog;
and Kinky Beard, guide the squad of ten.

Jock-cock come too, and Lowdown Dragon,
Pig Face with your tusks and Scratch Dog
and Butt-butterfly and crazy Redface.

Look all around the boiling dough;
make sure they're safe all the way to the next ridge
that goes all the way over the dens."

"Whoa, teacher, what's this I see?"
I said. "Uh, hey, let's go alone without an escort,
if you know the way; as far as I'm concerned, I don't ask
for one.

If you notice as much as you usually do,
don't you see that they're grinding their teeth,
and with their frowns, they're threatening to hurt us?"

And he to me: "I don't want you to be afraid;
let them grind to their hearts' content,
since they're doing it for the condemned ones in pain."

They took off to the left turn;
but first each pushed his tongue
to his teeth, toward their leader, as a signal;
and he made a trumpet out of his butthole.

Canto XXII

I've seen cavalry move camp
and start to storm and make their muster
and sometimes make their escape;

I've seen runners upon your land,
Aretines, and gangs of pillagers,
tournament teams and the running of jousts,

at times with trumpets, and bells,
with drums, and signals from the castle,
and with things domestic and foreign;

but never yet with such a strange bagpipe
have I seen horsemen or foot-soldiers move,
nor ships at a sign from earth or star.

We went with the ten demons.
What a fierce company! But in the church
with saints, and in the tavern with gluttons!

Purely on the tar-pit was my interest,
to see everything contained in the ditch
and the people on fire in it.

Like dolphins, when they make a sign
to sailors with the arcs of their backs
to pack up the ship,

so, to alleviate the pain,
some of the sinners would show their backs
and in less time hide it.

And as on the edge of water at a ditch
there are frogs with only their muzzles out,
hiding their feet and form,

everywhere there were sinners;
but as Kinky Beard approached,
they ducked back under the boiling.

I saw, and still my heart stutter-steps when I think of it,
one waiting, as perhaps
one frog remains and another jumps in;

and Scratch Dog, who was most across from him,
hooked him by his tarred hair
and pulled him up, looking to me like an otter.

I knew all their names by now,
since I made note of them when they were chosen,
and I listened to how they called each other.

"Hey, Redface, put
your nails at his back, so you can skin him!"
shouted all the cursed ones together.

And I: "My teacher, if you can,
find out who is this chump who
just came into his adversaries' hands."

My leader got close to him,
asked him where he was from, and he responded:
"I was born in the kingdom of Navarre.

132

My mother put me in the service of a landowner,
after she had me with a good-for-nothing
destroyer of himself and his things.

Then I joined the family of good king Tybalt;
there I set myself up to take bribes,
which is what I pay for in this heat."

And Pig-Face, from whose mouth came out
everywhere a tusk like a wild pig's,
made him feel how it could shred.

A mouse had come among bad cats;
but Kinky Beard closed him in his arms
and said: "Stop there, while I fork him."

And he turned his face to my teacher:
"Ask," he said, "more, if you want
to know more from him, before the others rip him to
shreds."

The leader then: "Now tell me: of the other wrongdoers,
do you know any who might be Latino
under the pitch?" And he: "I just left,

a little while ago, someone who was from near there.
I wish I were still covered over, beside him,
so I wouldn't have to fear fingernail or hook!"

And Jock-cock: "We have suffered too much,"
he said and seized his arm with the hook,
so that, yanking, he carried away from it a slice.

Lowdown Dragon, too, wanted to strike
at his legs; but their leader of the ten
turned around and around, facing them off.

When they were a little peaceful again,
of him who still stared at his wound
my leader didn't hesitate to demand:

"Who was that one unfortunately left behind
when you came ashore?"
And he responded: "It was Brother Gomita,

he of Gallura, purveyor of every fraud,
who had his boss's enemies in hand
and acted so that each one praised him.

He took money and let them off gently,
as he says; and in his other offices, too,
was not a minor crook but a king.

Sir Michel Zanche of Logodoro
hangs with him, and their tongues
never tire of talking about Sardinia.

Oh no. Look at that other one grinding his teeth;
I would say more, but I'm afraid that he's
arming himself to scratch my skin infection."

And the great officer turned to Butt-butterfly
who strained his eyes to strike,
and said: "Get control of yourself there, cursed
birdbrain!"

"If you want to see or hear,"
the frightened captive began again,
"Tuscans or Lombards, I'll make them come;

but the Evil Claws must stand a little back,
so that they won't be afraid of their spite;
and I, sitting in this same place,

for one of myself, will make seven come
when I whistle, as is our habit
to do when one of us gets himself out."

Dirty Dog at such a word lifted his muzzle,
shaking his head, and said: "Listen to the devilry
he has thought of, to throw himself down!"

And he, with a great store of traps,
responded: "I am too devilish
when I bring greater sadness on my own kind."

Bent Wing couldn't take any more, and opposing
the others, said to him: "If you get yourself back in,
I won't gallop after you,

but I'll beat my wings over the pitch.
Let's leave the hill, and the bank will be our shield,
to see if you alone are worth the rest of us."

And you who read will hear new sport:
each turned his eyes from the other side,
he first who wanted least to do it.

The Navarre man chose his time well,

made firm his feet on land, and in a split second
jumped and got himself free of their plans.

Each of them was suddenly struck with embarrassment,
but he who was the greatest reason for their defeat;
so he moved and shouted: "You're caught!"

It did him little good: wings
could not overtake terror. The other went under,
and that one turned his breast upward

not differently than the duck; suddenly,
when the falcon gets close and dives under,
it must fly back up, cross and broken.

Frost-stomper, irate at the trick,
flying close behind, hoped
that he would escape, to start a tussle.

Since the sinner had disappeared,
he turned his talons on his companion
and struggled with him above the pit.

But the other was quite a gryphon
and seized him well in his talons himself, and both of
them
fell in the middle of the stagnant boiling.

The heat made them let go of each other right away;
but they couldn't raise themselves,
the tar had so glued their wings.

Kinky Beard, wailing with the others,

sent four of them to fly to the other side
with their hooks, and quickly

from here, from there, they descended to their posts.
They put out their hooks toward the trapped ones,
who were already cooked into the crust.
And we left them in their frenzy.

Canto XXIII

Quiet, alone, without our company,
we went on, one in front and the other after,
as lesser monks go in the streets.

Aesop's fable was
on my mind
about the frog and the mouse;

the ideas of "now" and "this very hour" are not more alike
than one and the other, if one compares
the beginning and the end with fixed attention.

Just as one thought comes from another
born from that and then another,
the first fear now doubled for me.

I was thinking: "These guys
are fooled and hurt and made to look stupid,
and I'm sure it bothers them.

If outrage is added to their usual bad temper,
they'll come after us more viciously
than a dog mangles a rabbit."

I could already feel my hair curl
from fear, and I hung back
and said: "Teacher, if you don't hide yourself

and me right away, I'm scared
of the Evil Claws. They're already right behind us;
I imagine them so close I can feel them."

And he: "If I were a mirror made of leaded glass,
your outward image wouldn't reach
me faster than I'd reflect what's inside you.

Your thoughts have mixed with my own,
with a similar attitude and image,
so from both I've come up with one idea.

If the right bank lets us,
we can descend it into the next trench
and escape the chase we're imagining."

He hadn't finished telling me his idea
when I saw them coming with wings spread,
not far away, after us.

My leader quickly grabbed me
like a mother wakened by a noise
who sees flames burning near her

and grabs up her child and flees, not stopping,
more worried about him than about herself,
so she's only wearing her slip;

and down the hard bank,
stretched out, he slid on the hanging rock
that is one side of the next trench.

Water never ran so fast
toward the turning mill wheel
as it approaches the paddles

as my teacher down that border,
carrying me on his chest
like his son, not like his companion.

No sooner had his feet touched the bed
of the bottom below than they were at the hill
above us, but he wasn't afraid of them there;

high providence that
placed them as ministers of the fifth pit
takes away from them any power to leave it.

Down there we found painted people
who walked around with slow steps,
crying, tired and defeated.

They wore capes with hoods low
in front of their eyes, made like
those of the monks at Cluny.

Outside, they are covered with gold and shiny;
but inside they are all of lead, so heavy
that Federigo's cloaks would seem to be made of straw.

Wow, what an exhausting mantle!
We turned again to the left
together with them, listening to their sad cry.

Because of the weight, those tired people
moved so slowly that we had new
companions every time we moved a hip.

So I said to my leader: "Try to find

someone whose details or name you know,
just moving your eyes around."

And one of them who heard my Tuscan speech
from behind us shouted: "Stop your feet,
you who are running through this heavy air!

Maybe you can get from me what it is you want."
At which point the leader turned and said: "Wait,
and then walk at his pace."

I stopped and saw two showing great haste
of spirit in their faces, trying to get to me;
but they were held up by the weight and the narrowness
of the path.

When they reached me, with a suspicious eye
they looked at me without saying a word;
then they turned and said to each other:

"This one must be alive, the way his throat moves;
and if they're dead, what privilege
do they have not to be covered by the heavy stole?"

Then they said to me: "Hey, Tuscan
who's come to the meeting of sad hypocrites,
don't be too full of yourself to tell us who you are."

And I to them: "I was born and grew up
above the beautiful river Arno in the great city,
and I am in the body that I've always had.

But who are you people, so distilled

from what I see that the sadness runs down your cheeks?
And what suffering is in you that shines like that?"

And one answered me: "These orange capes
are of lead so heavy that the weight
makes their balances creak.

We were Knights of Our Lady from Bologna;
I am named Catalano, and this is Loderingo,
taken together by your land

as a single man who is usually chosen
to keep the peace; and we were so good at it
that it still shows around Gardingo."

I started: "Brothers, your bad deeds. . ."
but I said no more, for my eye was caught by
someone crucified to the ground with three stakes.

When he saw me, he contorted himself,
sighing into his beard;
and Brother Catalan, seeing this,

said to me: "This convict you are looking at
counseled the Pharisees that it would be better
to martyr one man for the people.

He is across the path naked,
as you see, and it is his job to feel
the weight of whoever passes, first.

And in this way his father-in-law is punished
in this pit, and the others of the council

that was, for the Jews, a bad seed."

Then I saw that Virgil marveled
over him who was stretched out on a cross
so vilely, in his eternal exile.

Then he voiced this to the Brother:
"May it not displease you, if you are allowed, to tell us
if on our right there is a passage

where we two can exit from here,
without having the black angels
come down here to get us out."

One replied then: "More close by than you can hope
is a stone that, from the great circle,
crosses all the ferocious valleys,

except here where it is broken and doesn't reach across;
but you can go up the ruin
that lies along the side and rises from the bottom."

The leader stayed a little while with his head bent down;
then he said: "Did he need to mislead us so badly,
the one who hooks the sinners over there?"

And the Brother: "I used to hear tell in Bologna
of the devil's many vices, among which I heard
that he is a liar and the father of lies."

Suddenly the leader left with great strides,
his face disturbed a little by rage;
I departed from the burdened ones

and followed behind the prints of his dear feet.

Canto XXIV

In that part of the young year
when the sun tempers its locks of hair beneath Aquarius
and the nights become half the day,

when the frost on the earth copies
the image of its white sister snow,
but its temperate pen doesn't last long,

the poor farmer, out of the supplies he needs,
gets up and looks around and sees the countryside
all white; so he hits his side,

goes back into the house, and here and there complains,
like a kid who doesn't know what to do;
then he laughs, and hope wins out again,

seeing the world with its changed face
in a little while, and he takes his hooked walking stick
and goes outside to drive his sheep to pasture.

So my teacher made me lose heart
when I saw his forehead so perturbed,
but as soon came the bandage to the wound.

As we came to the ruined bridge,
the leader turned to me with that sweet look
that I first saw at the foot of the mountain.

Arms open, after some thought,
first looking around
thoroughly at the ruin, he grasped me.

And as one who adapts and reconsiders,
who always thinks ahead,
so raising me up to the top

of a huge rock, he searched for another cliff,
saying: "Grab hold of that one;
but try it first to see if it can hold you."

This was not a path for those dressed in the cape,
and hardly for us; he lightweight and I being pushed,
we went up from jut to jut.

If it hadn't been that in that area
this side was shorter,
I don't know about him, but I would have been defeated.

But since the Evil Ditches all lean
toward the opening of the lowest well,
each valley carries

one side higher than the other descends;
we came to the end up at the point
where the last stone breaks off.

My lungs were so empty
when I got to the top that I could not go on,
and I sat the first chance I got.

"Now you have to hop to it,"
my teacher said; "because, sitting on feather pillows
and under quilts, you won't get famous;

without that, one's life is consumed;
what vestige is left on earth
is like smoke in the air or water in the sea spray.

So get up; beat this agony
with the spirit that wins every battle,
if it doesn't let its deadweight body drag it down.

There is still a longer stair to go up.
It's not enough to leave these guys behind.
If you understand me, try to benefit from it."

I got up then, showing myself fortified
with more breath than I felt,
and said: "Go on; I'm strong and determined."

We went on our way up the cliff,
which was broken, narrow and hard to make our way
along,
and much steeper than the one before.

I talked as I walked so I wouldn't seem worn out.
A voice came from the next ditch,
having trouble forming words.

I don't know what was said, though I was over the back
of the arch that bridges here;
but whoever was speaking seemed moved.

I had my face down, but my living eyes
couldn't go all the way to the bottom because it was so
dark;
so I said: "Teacher, you go

147

to the next circle and let's go down the wall;
what I hear from here I don't understand,
and what I see I can't figure out."

"Any other response," he said, "I won't give
except to get busy; an honest request
should be followed by silent action."

We went down the bridge to
where it reached the eighth bank,
and then I saw the ditch:

and I saw in there a terrible nest
of snakes so strange
that the memory freezes my blood.

No longer can Libya brag, with all its sand,
that it produces mythical monsters
like Amphisbaena,

nor of so many pestilent or virulent plagues
appearing in all of Ethiopia
or above the Red Sea.

Among this cruel and wretched plenty
ran naked frightened people,
without hope of a hole to hide in or a heliotrope to help
them disappear.

Their hands were tied behind them with snakes,
their tails and heads
twisted in front.

148

And there was one at our ledge
that a serpent struck at and transfixed
there, where the neck and shoulders knot.

Neither "O" nor "I" can be written so fast
as he caught on fire and burned, and
had to turn all to ashes, falling;

and then as he lay on the ground destroyed,
the powder gathered by itself
and became himself again.

This is, as the great wise ones confess,
how the phoenix dies and is reborn
when it approaches its five-hundredth year;

it doesn't graze on herbs and grains in its lifetime
but only on incense tears and cardamom spice,
and perfumes of nardo and myrrh are its funeral clothing.

And just like someone who faints and doesn't know why,
because demons pull him to the ground,
or that other illness that ties up a man

when he gets up and looks around,
all confused by the great anguish
he has suffered, and looking he sighs:

that's what that sinner was like after he got up.
God's power is so severe,
striking out in its vengeance!

The leader asked him then who he was;
so he answered: "I rained down from Tuscany
a little while ago, into this fierce gorge.

Bestial life pleased me, not human,
and I was like a mule; I am Vanni Fucci,
beast, and Pistoia was my den."

And I to the leader: "Tell him not to move,
and ask what sin pushed him down here;
I saw him as a man of blood and rage."

And the sinner, who heard, didn't fake
but directed at me his mind and face
and blushed with sad shame;

then said: "It hurts me more that you've caught me
in this misery where you see me
than when I was taken from that other life.

I can't deny what you ask;
I'm put so far down here because I
robbed the sacristy of its beautiful decorations

and falsely blamed someone else.
But so you don't enjoy this sight,
if you will ever get out of these dark places,

open your ears to my announcement, and listen.
Pistoia first will thin itself of the Black party;
then Florence will renew its people and parties.

The God of War draws up a vapor from the Valley of the

Magra River,
engulfed in turbid clouds;
and with a sudden violent storm,

battle will rage over Campo Piceno;
when suddenly the cloud will split
wounding every White party man.
I've told you this to give you pain."

Canto XXV

At the end of his words the thief
raised his hands with both the middle fingers,
screaming: "Take that, God! That's aimed at you."

From then on snakes were my friends,
because one turned itself around his neck,
as if to say "I don't want you to talk any more";

and another at his arms restrained him,
tying itself so in front
that he couldn't make a move.

Wow, Pistoia, Pistoia; why not just
burn yourself to ashes so that nothing's left,
since your descendants outdo you in evil?

In all the dark circles of Hell
I saw no spirit so arrogant against God,
not even the one who fell from the walls of Thebes.

He escaped without another word;
and I saw a centaur full of rage
come calling: "Where, where is that bitter one?"

I don't think Maremma has as many
snakes as he had on his back
down to his rump.

Over his shoulders, behind his neck,
lay a dragon with its wings spread,
setting fire to everything it came across.

My teacher said: "This is Cacus, who,
under the stone of the Aventine,
made many lakes of blood.

He's not on the same path as his brothers
because of the theft he fraudulently committed
of the great herd that was near him,

which ended his sneaky doings
under Hercules's mace, who maybe
hit him a hundred times, and he didn't feel the tenth."

While he talked like this, and he passed by,
three spirits came under us,
but neither I nor my leader noticed them

until they shouted: "Who are you guys?"
which made our story stop,
and then we listened only to them.

I didn't know them; but it happened,
as sometimes does,
that one had to say the other's name,

saying: "Where did Cianfa get left behind?"
so that I, to make sure my leader paid attention,
put my finger up from chin to nose.

If you are, reader, slow to believe
what I'm about to tell you, it's no wonder,
since I saw it, and even I can hardly believe it.

As I was standing there with raised eyebrows,
a serpent with six feet throws itself
in front of one of them and fastens all on him.

With its middle feet it clamped his belly
and with the front legs it pinned his arms;
and sank its teeth into one cheek after the other;

it stretched its hind feet down his thighs,
and put its tail between them
and stretched it behind him above his rear.

Barbed ivy was never
so stuck to a tree as the horrible beast
was to the other's limbs.

Then they stuck like hot wax
might and mixed their color,
so neither one looked like what he was,

as, before the flame,
a brown color proceeds along the papyrus
that isn't black, yet the white dies.

The other two watched him, and each
screamed: "Oh my, Agnello, you're changing!
Look at how you're not two things or one!"

Already the two heads had become one
when it seemed the two faces mixed
into one face, and the two were lost.

Two arms were made of four limbs;

154

the thighs and legs and the belly and the chest
turned into body parts never seen before.

Every original aspect was cancelled;
the perverse image appeared two and no one
and, like that, left with slow steps.

As a lizard under the great whip
of the dog days moving between hedges
crosses the road like lightning,

so appeared, coming toward the bellies
of the other two, a fiery serpent,
livid and black like pepper;

and on that part where we take
food, it attached itself to one of them
and then fell down along the front of him.

The transfixed one looked at it but said nothing;
instead, with his feet still, he yawned
as if sleep or fever assaulted him.

He and the serpent gazed at each other;
one's wound and the other's mouth
smoked, and the smoke blew together.

Hush, Lucan, talking
about the misery of Sabellus and Nasidius,
and wait to hear what erupts now.

Ovid, be quiet about Cadmus and Arethusa
because, if he turns into a serpent and she into a fountain

for poetic license, you have nothing on my story;

for two natures never front to front
transformed the two
and were so ready to exchange the stuff they were made
of.

They responded together
so the serpent split its tail into a fork,
and the wounded one pulled his feet back together.

The legs and the thighs
were so attached that soon the joining
would leave no sign of itself.

The tail took the figure
that the other one lost there, and his skin
became soft and the other's hard.

I saw the arms enter the armpits,
and the beast's two feet, that were short,
become as long as the other's shortened.

Then the back feet, twisted together,
became the member that the man hides,
and of his own the miserable man now carried two.

While the smoke veils one and the other
with new color, and grows hair on one part
and takes it from another,

one rose up and the other fell down,
not turning away the blasphemous glittering eyes

under which each changed his muzzle.

The one upright drew it toward the temples,
and from too much material
came ears from the empty cheeks;

what did not run back and was left
of that excess made a nose on the face,
and the lips thickened as much as they needed.

The muzzle is chased forward from the one lying down,
and the ears pull back to the head
like a snail pulls in its horns;

and the tongue, that was united and able
before to speak, splits, and the fork
of the other closes; and the smoke ends.

The soul that became a beast,
hissing, takes off through the valley,
and the other spits after him, speaking.

Then he turned his new shoulders
and said to the other: "I want Buoso to run,
as I have done, crawling on this road."

So I saw the seventh ballast
mutate and transform; and here I excuse myself
with the newness of it, if my pen has made a mess of it.

And even if my eyes were confused
somewhat and my mind blown,
they could not escape so sneakily

that I couldn't pretty well make out Puccio Sciancato;
and only he, of the three companions
who first came, wasn't changed;
the other was the one that you, Gaville, mourn.

Canto XXVI

Celebrate, Florence, that you are so great
that by sea and by land you beat your wings,
and your name spreads throughout Hell!

Between the thieves you will find five of
your citizens who shame me,
and they haven't made you very praiseworthy.

But if we dream the truth as morning comes,
you will soon feel
what Prato, if no one else, wants for you.

And if it already were, it wouldn't be too soon.
If only it were, as it needs to be!
It will weigh me down more, the older I get.

We left there, and up the stairs
that turned us white as ivory when we first came down,
my leader went up and brought me,

and following the solitary way,
between the jagged stone and among the cliff rocks,
our feet couldn't move without our hands.

Then I was sorry, and now I'm sorry again,
when I thought of what I saw,
and I hide my genius more than usual

so it won't run where virtue doesn't guide it;
so, if a good star or some better luck
gives me its benefit, I won't be ungrateful.

Like the poor farmer who rests on a hill
when the sun that lights the world
keeps its face the least hidden from us,

when the fly gives way to the mosquito,
and he sees fireflies down in the valley
as he plows in the vineyard,

resplendent with so many flames
was the eighth ditch, as I realized
as soon as I was where the floor appeared.

And like the man avenged by the bears
who saw Elijah's chariot departing,
when the horses reared and rose to the sky,

but he could follow nothing with his eyes
and saw nothing but the single flame
going up like a little cloud,

so each moves along the throat
of the pit, so that none reveals the theft
as each flame steals a sinner.

I stood up straight on the bridge to see,
so that if I hadn't grabbed a big rock,
I would have fallen down without being pushed.

And the leader, who saw me so interested,
said: "Inside those fires are the spirits;
each one makes himself into what is burning him."

"My teacher," I responded, "hearing you
makes me more certain; but already I thought
that's what it might be, and I already wanted to say to
you:

who is in that fire so split
at the top as to surge from the pyre
where Eteocles was put with his brother?"

He responded to me: "In there suffer
Ulysses and Diomedes, and so together
revenge comes as does rage;

and inside their flame they regret
the scheme of the horse that was the door
where the noble seed of Rome would spill out.

They cry about the craftiness that, dead,
Deidamia still mourns for Achilles,
and they carry their punishment for the Palladium in
there."

"If they inside those flames
speak," I said, "teacher, and I ask
and ask again, a thousand times asking,

don't deny my waiting until
the horned flame gets here;
you see desire makes me lean toward it!"

And he to me: "Your request is worthy
of a lot of praise, and I accept it;
but hold your tongue.

Let me do the talking, since I understand
what you want; they might resist,
since they were Greeks, whatever you say."

Then the flame came near
where it appeared to my leader the time and place,
and I heard him speak like this:

"You who are two in one fire,
if I deserved your respect while I lived,
if I deserved a little or a lot of respect

when I wrote high verses in the world,
then don't move away; but one of you say
where, lost, he went to die."

The bigger horn of the ancient flame
started to roil and murmur,
like one wiped out by the wind;

the tip waved here and there like a weapon,
as if it were the tongue that spoke
and threw out a voice that said: "When

I left Circe, who kept me
more than a year there near Gaeta,
before Aeneas named it,

neither a son's love nor respect
for my old father, not even the loving debt
I owed Penelope, to make her happy,

could defeat the ardor inside me
that I had to know the world
and men's strengths and weaknesses;

but I put myself on the high open sea
alone with a ship and that company
of a few who had not deserted me.

I saw one shore and the other all the way to Spain,
as far as Morocco and the island of Sardegna
and the other islands bathed in that sea.

I and the company were old and slow
when we came to that narrow opening
where Hercules marked his sites,

warning men not to set foot;
on the right hand I left Seville,
and on the other I'd already left Setta.

'Hey, brothers,' I said, 'who through a thousand dangers
have reached Europe,
with this little awareness

that remains of our senses,
you don't want to waste this experience,
following the sun, of the unpopulated world.

Consider your seed:
you weren't made to live like animals,
but to go after virtue and knowledge.'

I got my companions so excited

with this little speech, for the trip,
that I could barely have held them back;

and having turned our rear deck to the morning,
we made our oars into wings in our mad flight,
always gaining on the left.

All the stars of the other pole already saw the night,
and ours were so low
that they didn't rise above the ocean floor.

Five times relit and as many times put out
the light under the moon,
since we'd entered the deep pass,

when a mountain appeared, brown
in the distance, and it appeared to me so high
I'd never seen anything like it.

Our celebration soon turned to grief;
from the new land a whirlwind was born
that ran into the front of the ship.

Three times it turned with all the water;
and the fourth lifted the rear up
and the prow went down, as someone willed it,
until the sea closed over us."

Canto XXVII

The flame stood straight up and quiet
to say no more, and was already leaving us,
with the sweet poet's permission,

when another coming behind it
made us turn our eyes to its tip
because of the confused sound that came out of it.

As the Sicilian bull that first bellowed
with the cry of him, as was right,
who had made it with his file,

bellowed with the voice of the afflicted,
so that, although it was made of brass,
it seemed transfixed by suffering,

so, not having a path nor a form
to start with in the fire, in its language
the miserable words changed.

But once they made their journey
up through the tip, giving it that quiver
that they had given the tongue as they passed,

we heard it say: "You who I aim
my voice at and who speak like a Lombard,
saying 'Now go, as I don't require anything more of you,'

though I've probably gotten here a little bit late,
don't get annoyed about staying to talk to me;
you see I'm not annoyed, and I'm burning!

If you've just fallen into this blind world
from the sweet Latin land
from where I've brought all my sin,

tell me if the Romagnians have peace or war;
I'm from where the mountains are between Urbino
and the Tyber's dam."

I was still listening and bending forward
when my leader poked my side
saying: "You speak, this one's Italian."

And I, already having an answer ready,
without waiting to speak, began:
"Soul hidden down there,

your Romagna isn't and never was
free of war in its tyrants' hearts:
but I didn't leave any open fighting there.

Ravenna is as it has been for many years:
Polenta's eagle broods there
so that it covers Cervia with its wings.

The land that already made it through the long test
and made of the French a bloody pile
finds itself again under the green claws.

And the old mastiff and the new of Verruchio,
who handled Montagna badly,
there sharpen their teeth.

The cities of Lamone and Santerno
conduct the lion from the white nest,
changing from summer to winter.

And the one whose side the Savio bathes,
just as it lies between the flatland and the mountain,
is between tyranny and the free state.

Now, who are you, I ask you to tell us;
don't be harder on others than another's been,
so your name can go on in the world."

Then when the fire had roared
a while in its way, the sharp point moved
here and there and then breathed:

"If I believed that my answer would be
made to a person who would ever return to the world,
this flame would never more burn;

but since from this depth
no one has ever returned alive, if I hear the truth,
without fear of disgrace, I answer you.

I was a man of arms and then a corded monk,
believing myself, belted like that, to make amends;
and certainly my belief would have been fulfilled

if it had not been for a great priest—may evil take him!—
who took me back to my old sins;
and how and why I'd like you to listen to.

While I was formed of the bone and the flesh

167

that my mother gave me, my acts
were not those of the lion but those of the fox.

The schemes and sneaky ways, I knew them all,
and so practiced their skills
that noise of it went out to the ends of the earth.

When I had reached that
age where everyone should
lower the sails and coil up the ropes,

what used to please me then disgusted me,
and I gave myself to penance and confession;
oh misery is mine! It could've worked!

The prince of the new Pharisees
made war near Laterano
and not with the Saracens or Jews,

so all his enemies were Christian,
and none went to conquer Akká
nor to be a merchant in the land of the Sultan;

neither highest office nor sacred vows
were kept by him, nor by me in that belt
used to keep its wearers thin.

But as Constantine asked Sylvester
from Mount Soracte to cure him of leprosy,
so I was asked as an expert

to cure him of his feverish pride,
he asking my counsel, and I silent

because his words seemed drunken.

And then he asked again: 'Don't let your heart doubt;
I absolve you if you will teach me to
throw Palestrina to the ground.

I can lock and unlock Heaven, as you know;
but these are two keys
that the Pope before me didn't value.'

Then his weighty arguments
made me think silence was my worst choice,
and I said: 'Father, since you cleanse me

of the sin that it falls to me to commit,
a long promise with a short wait
will make you triumph on the high throne.'

St. Francis came for me when I was dead;
but one of the black angels told him:
'Don't take him; don't wrong me.

He must come down among my homeboys
for the false counsel he gave;
from that to this state, I've stayed in his hair;

no one's absolved without repentance,
and one can't repent and will an act together at the same
time,
for the contradiction gives no consent.'

Oh, the pain I'm in! How I shuddered
when he seized me, saying: 'Maybe

you didn't think I'd know logic.'

He carried me to Minos; and that one coiled
his tail eight times around his hard back;
and then in his great rage bit it,

and said: 'This one is for the thieves' fire';
so I'm here where you see me lost,
covered in this, wandering, grieving."

When he had concluded what he had to say,
the weeping flame departed,
twisting and pulsing its sharp horn.

We kept going, my leader and I,
up the cliff to the other arch
that covers the ditch where they pay the fine
for disunity by earning this burden.

Canto XXVIII

Who could even with free verse
tell fully of the blood and the wounds
that I saw now, describing it over and over again?

Every tongue would certainly come up short
because our speech and thought
have little heart to comprehend so much.

If all the people assembled again
who already on the fated land
of Puglia mourned for their blood

that the Trojans and the long war
spilled, and stripped their rings,
as Livy writes, who makes no mistakes,

with those who felt the painful beating
they got when they resisted Robert Guiscard,
and the others whose bones are still piled

at Ceperano, there where each Puglia man lied
like the men from Tagliacozzo,
where the old Alardo won without weapons,

and one shows a pierced limb and one cut off,
it would be nothing compared
to the foulness of the ninth ditch.

A wine keg was
never so split open as one guy I saw
broken from his chin to where he farts.

171

Between his legs hung his intestines;
I saw his heart and the sorry sack
that turns what one swallows into shit.

While I was all caught up looking at him,
he looked at me and with his hands opened his chest,
saying: "Now see how I rip into myself!

See how torn is Muhammad!
In front of me goes weeping Ali,
his face broken from chin to brow.

And all the others you see here,
spreaders of scandal and division
while alive, and so torn apart.

A devil is back there who splits us
so cruelly, a cut of the sword
again for each of this gang

when we have gone around this sad street;
but the wounds close
before we go in front of him again.

But who are you meditating up there on the cliff,
maybe to put off going to the penalty
judged up there for what you're accused of?"

"Death hasn't reached him yet, and guilt didn't bring
him,"
responded my teacher, "to be tormented;
but to give him full experience,

I, who am dead, must lead him
through Hell from circle to circle;
and this is as true as it is that I am speaking to you."

Then more than a hundred, hearing this,
stopped in the ditch to look at me
in amazement, forgetting their pain.

"Now tell Father Dolcin to arm himself,
you who might see the sun soon,
if he doesn't want to follow me here right away,

with enough food that the snow's siege
doesn't hand victory to the Novarese,
that otherwise would not be so easy to get."

With one foot up,
Muhammad spoke to me this word;
then he put it on the ground and kept going.

Another who had his throat run through
and his nose split to the eyebrows
and nothing but one ear left,

rested to look in wonder
with the others; in front of the others opened his throat,
which was red everywhere,

and said: "You, not condemned by guilt
and who I saw in the Latin land of Italy,
if I'm not fooled by your resemblance,

173

remember Pier da Medicina,
if you ever return to see the sweet plain
that runs from Vercelli to Marcabò.

And let the two best men in Fano know,
Mister Guido and also Angiolello,
that, unless the foresight here is wrong,

they'll be thrown out of their ship
and killed near La Cattolica
because of a foul tyrant's betrayal.

Between the islands of Cyprus and Majorca,
Neptune, the God of the Sea, never saw so vile a deed,
not by pirates, and not by Greeks.

That traitor who sees with one eye
and rules the land that one here with me
wishes he'd starved before seeing,

will have them come to talk with him;
then he will act so that the wind of Focara
won't be stopped by their promises or prayers."

And I to him: "Show me and tell me,
if you want me to carry up your news,
who is the one with this bitter vision."

Then he put his hand on the jaw
of one of his companions and opened the mouth,
shouting: "This is he, but he doesn't talk.

This one, chased out, put down all

174

Caesar's doubts, affirming that an armed man
always is harmed by delay."

Oh, how anguished he seemed to me
with his tongue cut in his throat,
Curio, such a bold speaker!

And another with his hands cut off
lifted the stumps in the thick air,
and with blood making his face filthy,

screamed: "Remember The Fly, too,
who said, 'What's done is done,'
who was an evil seed for the Tuscan people."

And I added: "And of death to your line";
so that he, piling anguish upon suffering,
left like someone saddened and maddened.

But I remained to watch the crowd
and saw something that I would be afraid,
without more proof, even to talk about;

if my conscience didn't reassure me,
the good companion that strengthens a man
under the armor of feeling pure.

I certainly saw, and still seem to see,
a headless body walking like
the others in that miserable gang;

the trunk held the head by its hair,
swinging from the hand like a lantern:

and it saw us and said: "Oh, my!"

He had made a lamp of himself,
and they were two in one and one in two;
how this can be, he knows who makes it so.

When he was right at the foot of the bridge,
he raised high the arm with the head
to bring his words closer to us,

which were: "Now see the painful penalty,
you who, breathing, go seeing the dead:
do you see anything as great as this?

And since you may carry back news of me,
know that I am Bertram dal Bornio,
he who gave the young king bad advice.

I made the father and the son rebel against each other.
Ahithophel did no more with Absalom
and David with his evil insinuations.

Since I parted two people in unity,
I carry my brain severed, oh grief,
from its origin here in this body.
So you see in me that what goes around comes around."

Canto XXIX

The many people and their different wounds
made my eyes so drunk
that they wanted to stay and weep.

But Virgil said to me: "What are you staring at?
Why is your sight so fixed down there
among the sad, hacked up shadows?

You haven't done this at the other ditches;
think, if you plan to count them off,
that the valley is twenty-two miles around.

And already the moon is below our feet;
there is little time left to us,
and there is more to see that you don't see."

"If you had," I suddenly responded,
"paid attention to why I'm looking,
maybe you would have let me stay longer."

He departed, and I went behind him,
already making a response to the leader,
and adding: "Inside that cave

where my eyes were so fixated,
I think the spirit of my blood relative
cries for the sin that costs so much down there."

Then the teacher said: "Don't let him break
into your thoughts from here on out.
Think of other things, and leave him be;

because I saw him at the foot of the little bridge
point at you and threaten you strongly with his finger,
and I heard him called Beautiful Jerry.

You were so completely worked up
over that guy who held the High Fort
that you didn't look over there, so he left."

"My leader, his violent death
that still isn't avenged," I said,
"by anyone who might share the shame of it

made him disdainful; so he went
without speaking to me, I think;
and that made me pity him more."

So we talked until we reached the first place
on the cliff that showed us the other valley,
if there'd been more light, all the way to the bottom.

When we were above the last cloister
of the Evil Ditches and all of its converts
could appear to our view,

a deluge of lamenting shot me through
like arrows tipped with pity;
so I covered my ears with my hands.

What suffering there would be, if from the hospitals
of Valdichiana between June and September
and of Maremma and Sardegna, the ill

were in a pit all together,
that's what was there, and the stink that escaped
was what comes from rotting limbs.

We went down to the last bank
of the long cliff, keeping left;
and then my view was more vivid

down to the bottom, there where the minister
of the high infallible God of justice
punishes the counterfeiters here recorded.

I don't believe greater sadness was seen
when the people of Aegina were all sick,
when the air was so full of illness

that the animals, down to the smallest worm,
all fell, and then the old people,
according to what the poets affirm,

were restored by ants' eggs,
than to see into that dark valley
spirits languishing in piles.

Some on the bellies and some on the backs of others
stretched out, and some crawled
on hands and knees along the sad street.

Step by step we went without speaking,
looking and listening to the sick,
who couldn't lift their bodies.

I saw two sitting leaned against each other,

as if heating up platter to platter,
from head to foot spotted with scabs;

and I never saw a curry comb moved
by a boy whose employer is waiting,
or one who has had to miss his sleep,

like each of these often dug
his nails across himself because of the great raging
itch that had no other cure;

and the fingernails pulled down the scabs,
like the knife that strips
fish with large scales.

"Hey, you stripping off your coat of mail with your
fingers,"
began my leader to one of them,
"and making pincers of them sometimes,

tell us if there are any Italians among them
in here, and may your fingernails last you
eternally at that work."

"We are Latin, who you see wasted
here, both of us," responded one, crying;
"but who are you, asking us?"

And the leader said: "I'm one who descends
with this living man down from ledge to ledge,
so I can show him Hell."

Then they broke their common propping up;

180

and each trembling turned to me
as did the others who'd overheard.

The good teacher pulled me all up close to him,
saying: "Tell them what you want";
and I started, since this was what he wanted:

"So your memory doesn't get lost in the first world
from the minds of men,
but so it lives under many suns,

tell me who you are and from what people;
don't let your foul and fastidious punishment
make you afraid to show yourselves to me."

"I am from Arezzo, and Albero of Siena,"
responded one, "had me burned alive;
but what I died for didn't bring me here.

It's true I said to him, speaking as a joke:
'I know how to rise in the air and fly';
and he, who had great will but little wisdom,

asked me to show him the skill; and only
because I didn't make him Daedalus, he had me
burned by one he considered his son.

But in the last ditch of the ten,
because of the alchemy I used in the world,
Minos, who is never mistaken, damned me."

And I said to the poet: "Were there ever
people as vain as those of Siena?

Certainly not even the French!"

At which point the other leper, listening to me,
responded to what I'd said: "Except for Stricca,
who knew how to spend temperately,

and Niccolò, whose rich custom
of cloves first started
in the grove where that seed germinated;

and for the gang that wasted
Hunter of Ascian's vineyards and great fields,
and The Howler gave a piece of his mind.

But to let you know who's got your back
against the Sienese, get a good look at me,
so my face can give you your answer:

you'll see I'm Top Eye's shadow,
who falsified metals with alchemy;
and you'll remember, if I've judged you correctly,
how I was a good ape of nature."

Canto XXX

In the time when the goddess Juno was outraged
by Semele against the Theban blood,
as she had already shown again and again,

Atamas became so insane,
seeing his wife with two children
walking encumbered by each holding a hand,

he shouted: "Spread the nets so I can catch
the lioness and her cubs as they pass";
and he stretched out his pitiless claws,

seizing the one they'd named Learchus,
and spun him and slammed him on a stone;
and she drowned herself with her other charge.

And when fortune brought down
the Trojans, all bold, from their high
so that together the kingdom and the king were crushed,

Hecuba, sad, miserable, and a captive,
then saw Polyxena killed,
and saw her Polydorus down on the shore

of the sea, the grieving woman
out of her mind barked like a dog,
so much had her grief twisted her mind.

But no Theban Furies or Trojans
seemed as cruel in going after beasts,
let alone human limbs,

as I saw two naked pale shadows
that ran biting like
pigs when the pigsty is opened.

One reached Top Eye and by the nape
of his neck gored him so that, pulling,
it dragged him on his belly over the hard ground.

And the Aretine, left behind trembling,
said to me: "That crazy soul is Gianni Schicchi,
and he goes rabidly like that after others."

"Oh," I said to him, "may it never fix
its teeth in you; please don't be too sick and tired
to tell me who it is, before it gets away."

And he to me: "That's the ancient soul
of shameless Myrrha, who became
to her father, more than was right, his friend.

She came to him to sin,
faking another's appearance,
as did the other getting away there,

to gain the lady of the herd,
pretend to be Buoso Donati,
drawing up a will and testifying to its validity."

And when the two rabid spirits had passed
that I'd been keeping an eye on,
I turned to look at the others born in evil.

I saw one made like a lute,
as if he'd been cut off
where a man's body splits in two.

The heavy dropsy, bloating
the limbs with stagnant fluids
so that the face doesn't match the belly,

made him keep his lips open
as a feverish person does, thirsty,
with one lip toward the chin and the other twisted up.

"You guys who are without any punishment,
I don't know why, in this miserable world,"
he said to us, "look and pay attention

to the anguish of Mister Adam;
I had in life all I wanted,
and now, oh despair, I wish for a drop of water.

The streams in the green hills of Casentino
flowing down to the Arno,
making their canals cold and soft,

are always in front of me, and not for nothing
does their image dry me up
more than the illness that distorts my face.

Rigid justice that teases me
uses the place where I sinned
to put more of my sighs to flight.

There where Romena is, I falsified

the money stamped with John the Baptist;
for that I left my body up there, burned.

But if I could have seen down here the sad soul
of Guido or of Alessandro or of their brother,
I wouldn't give up that sight for Fonte Branda.

One is in here with us already, if the raging
spirits who move around us tell the truth;
but what use is that to me, with my limbs tied?

If only I were light enough
that I could in a hundred years move an inch,
I would have already started on my way,

looking for him among this squalid people,
though this ditch runs eleven miles
and stretches not less than half a mile across.

I am because of them among such a family;
they made me strike the coins
that had three carats of dirt."

And I to him: "Who are the two
who smoke like wet hands in winter,
lying stretched out close by your right hand?"

"I found them here—and since then they haven't turned—
"
he responded, "when I rained down into this ditch,
and I don't think they will for all eternity.

One is the woman who falsely accused Joseph;

186

the other is the false Sinon, the Greek from Troy:
their sharp fever makes them throw off so much stink."

And one of them, annoyed
maybe at being named so unattractively,
hit with his fist the stretched gut.

It sounded like a drum;
and Mister Adam hit the face with his arm,
that seemed no less hard,

saying to him: "Still though I may seem unable
to move because my legs are heavy,
I have an arm free enough for that job."

And he responded: "When you went
to the fire, your arm was not so ready;
but it was all that and more when you were coining."

And the man with dropsy: "You speak the truth about
this:
but you weren't such an honest witness
when you were asked at Troy."

"If I spoke falsely, you faked the coins,"
said Sinon; "and I am here for one fault,
and you for more than any other demon!"

"Remember, perjurer, the horse,"
responded the one who had the inflated gut;
"and regret that the whole world knows about it!"

"And may you regret the thirst that's splitting,"

said the Greek, "your tongue, and the filthy water
that swells your gut like a bush in front of your eyes!"

Then the moneymaker: "So
your mouth hangs open for filth, as usual;
if I'm thirsty and fluid-stuffed,

you have fever and a headache,
and licking Narcissus's mirror
wouldn't take much invitation."

I was intent on listening to them
when my teacher said to me: "Now keep watching,
and it won't take much for me to pick a fight with you!"

When I heard him speak to me with anger,
I turned toward him with shame
that still plays back in my memory.

Like a man who dreams that he is hurt,
and dreaming wants to dream,
wanting what is as though it weren't,

so was I, unable to speak,
wanting to excuse myself, and excusing
myself all along, and not thinking that I did it.

"Less shame would wash away a greater defect,"
said my teacher, "than yours was;
so unburden yourself of every sorrow.

And think that I am always at your side,
if it happens again that chance takes hold of you

where there are people in a similar fight:
desiring to hear such things is a low desire."

Canto XXXI

The same tongue that bit me
so that each of my cheeks colored
then gave me the medicine;

as I've heard that the same spear
of Achilles and his father was the cause
first of a sad and then of a good gift.

We turned our backs to the wretched valley
up the bank that belts it,
crossing without speaking.

Here it was less than night and less than day,
so that I could not see far ahead;
but I heard a horn blow

so loudly that it would have made thunder quiet,
so that, instead of following the path,
I directed my eyes all at one place.

After the sad defeat, when
Charlemagne lost the holy knights,
Roland did not sound so terrifying.

I'd looked that way only a short while
when I saw a lot of high towers;
and I: "Teacher, tell me, what land is this?"

And he to me: "Because you look through
the shadows from too far away,
you mistake what you see.

You will see well when you get there,
because the sense fools itself from far away;
so push yourself that much more."

Then lovingly he took me by the hand
and said: "Before we travel further on,
so the fact won't appear strange to you,

know that these are not towers but giants,
and they are in the well around the bank
from the navel down, all of them."

As when clouds dissipate,
the sight little by little reconfigures
what was hidden by the vapor that thickened the air;

so seeing through the thick, dark air,
drawing closer and closer to the edge,
error fled me and fear grew

because, like the circle of
Montereggioni's crown of towers,
so at the bank that circles the well

half the bodies towered
of the horrible giants Jehovah menaces
from the sky when he thunders.

And I could make out the face of one,
the shoulders and chest and a lot of the stomach,
and at his sides both his arms.

Surely nature when she gave up the art
of making such creatures did well
to take such executioners from the God of War.

And if her elephants and whales
do not make her repent, if one looks subtly,
she will seem more just and more careful;

for where the argument of the mind
is added to evil will and power,
there is no refuge for the people.

His face seemed to me long and huge
like the pine at Saint Peter's in Rome,
and his other bones were in proportion;

so that the bank, which was a cover
from his middle downwards, showed so much
above that to reach to the crown of his hair

three Frieslanders might brag for nothing;
because I saw three huge spans of him
below where men fasten their cloak.

"Rafael evil friends goats souls"
the savage mouth began to shout
which was not fit for sweeter psalms.

And my leader to him: "Idiot soul,
stick with your trumpet, and use that to express yourself
when rage or other passions touch you!

Search at your neck, and you'll find the cord

that ties it, confused soul,
and you'll see it holds back your enormous chest."

Then he said to me: "He accuses himself;
this is Nimrod whose evil cost
the world one language no longer used.

Leave him there, and let's not speak to emptiness,
because to him every language is like his is to others,
so that nothing is understood."

We then travelled on,
turned to the left; and as far as a bolt shot from a
crossbow,
we found another more ferocious and huge.

Who might have had the skill to tie him,
I can't say, but one arm was tied
in front of him and the right behind

by a chain that held him
from the neck down, so we could see
it wound around him five times.

"This arrogant one wanted to exert
his power against the highest Jehovah,"
said my guide, "so he merits this.

His name is Ephialtes, and he made the great assault
when the giants frightened the gods;
the arms he threatened them with will never move again."

And I to him: "If it's okay,

I'd like the immeasurable Briareus
to be experienced by my own eyes."

And he responded: "You'll see Antaeus
close to here; he speaks and isn't restrained,
so he'll put us at the bottom of all sin.

The one you want to see is much farther on
and is tied and made like this one,
except more ferocious in the face."

Never was an earthquake more robust
that shook a tower as strongly
as Ephialtes soon shook himself.

Then I feared more than I had ever feared death,
and no more was needed to grant it to me,
if I had not seen his restraints.

We proceeded ahead,
and we saw Antaeus, a good fifteen feet,
not counting his head, above the cave.

"You who in the fortunate valley
that made Scipio glory's heir,
when Hannibal and his men turned their backs,

you took a thousand lions as prey,
so that, if you'd been at the great war
of your brothers, still it is believed

the sons of the earth would have won;
place us down there, and don't refuse it,

where Cocytus, the Lake of Lamentation, is sealed in by
cold.

Don't make us go to Tityus or Typhon;
this man can give you what you want,
so bend down and don't sneer.

He can still make you famous in the world
because he lives, and a long life awaits him
if the Graces don't call him before his time is up."

So the teacher spoke; and the other quickly
reached out his hands and took my leader
in the tight grip felt before by Hercules.

Virgil, when he felt himself taken,
said to me: "Here, let me take you";
then he made a bundle of himself and me.

When one sees the Garisenda, the Tower of Pisa,
under the leaning side, when a cloud goes
over it, it seems to hang from it:

so Antaeus seemed to me as I stayed still to stare
and see him bend, and that was when
I wished I'd gone by some other way.

But lightly at the bottom that devours
Lucifer and Judas, he set us down;
nor, in bending, did he hang around,
and like a mainmast in a ship he rose.

Canto XXXII

If I had bitter, rough rhymes,
like this sad hole needs,
with all the other rocks bridging it,

I would squeeze out the juice of my concept
more fully; but since I don't have them,
I go on but not without fear;

because it's not an enterprise to take on as a joke,
to describe the bottom of the universe,
and not for a tongue calling out "Mama" and "Daddy."

But those Muse ladies helping my verse
helped Amphion to wall in Thebes,
so that the fact and the telling are no different.

Oh, most badly conceived nobodies
who dwell in the place hard to talk about,
better you'd been sheep or goats!

As we were down in the dark well
far below the giant's feet,
and I still gazed at the high wall,

I heard a voice say to me: "Watch where you walk:
go so you don't step
on the heads of the miserable, tired brothers."

So I turned, and I saw ahead
and under the feet a lake whose ice
was like glass and not like water.

So thick a veil didn't run its course
in the winter at Austria's Danube
or the Don beneath the cold sky,

as it was here; if the Tambernic
had fallen on it, or the Pietrapana,
even the edge wouldn't have creaked.

And as the frog sits and croaks
with its muzzle out of the water, when
the farm woman often dreams of gleaning,

livid, down to where shame appears,
were lamenting spirits in the ice,
their teeth like a stork's song.

Each turned down its face;
their cold mouths and their sad eyes
among them were their testimony.

When I had looked around me for a while,
I turned to my feet and saw two so entangled
the hair on their heads mixed together.

"Tell me, you with your chests pressed together,"
I said, "who are you?" And they strained their necks;
and then when they'd raised their faces to me,

their eyes, that were at first wet inside,
spilled drops down on their lips, and the ice seized
the tears between them and sealed them together again.

Wood to wood was never nailed
so hard; and they like two rams
butted heads, so much rage overtook them.

And one who'd lost both ears
to frostbite, with his face lowered,
said: "Why do you stare at us like a mirror?

If you want to know who those two are,
the valley where Bisenzo runs down
once belonged to their father, Alberto, and to them.

They came from one body; and all of Caina
could be searched, and you wouldn't find a shadow
more worthy to be stuck in an ice cream:

not the one whose chest and shadow were broken
when Arthur's hand hit him;
not Focaccia; not the one blocking me

with his head so I can't see past him,
and who was named Sassol Mascheroni;
if you're Tuscan, you know quite well who he was.

And so you don't get me to go on talking,
know that I was Camiscion of the Crazies;
and I wait for Carlin to clear me."

Then I saw a thousand faces hangdog
from the cold; and I shivered,
and always will at icy ponds.

And while we walked toward the center

where all heavy things come together,
I trembled in the eternal cool;

if it was freewill, destiny, or chance,
I don't know, but walking among the heads,
I kicked one in the face.

Crying, he screamed at me: "Why are you bothering me?
If you haven't come to get more revenge
for Montaperti, why molest me?"

And I: "My teacher, wait for me now,
so I can take care of a doubt I have about this one;
and then I'll hurry as much as you want."

The leader stopped, and I said to him
who was still shrieking obscenities:
"Which one are you, to carry on like that against others?"

"Now who are you to go through Antenora
kicking," he responded, "other people's jaws,
especially since, if I were alive, this would be too much?"

"I'm alive, and it may be precious to you,"
was my response; "if you want fame;
I could put your name among the others I've made a note
of."

And he to me: "Just the opposite is what I want.
Get out of here, and don't give me any more grief;
you don't even know how to kiss up down here."

Then I grabbed him by the back of his scalp

and said: "Either you tell me your name
or you won't have any hair left up here."

And he to me: "You can make me bald,
and I won't tell you who I am or show you,
if you throw yourself on my head a thousand times."

I already had his hair twisted in my hand,
and had just pulled out more than one lock of it,
while he howled with his eyes looking down,

when another hollered: "What's with you, Mouth?
Isn't it enough clacking your jaws,
but now you've got to howl, too? What devil's got his
hands on you?"

"Now," I said, "I don't need to hear any more,
wicked traitor; to your shame,
I'll carry back true news about you."

"Go away," he said, "and tell whatever you want to;
but don't stay quiet, if you ever get out of here,
about the one whose tongue was so quick just now.

Here he cries about the Frenchmen's silver:
'I saw,' you can say, 'the guy from Duera
there where the sinners stay cool.'

And if you're asked 'Who else was there?'
beside you is someone from Beccheria
whose throat Florence slit.

I believe Gianni de' Soldanier is

200

further on with Ganellone and Tebaldello,
who unlocked Faenza while it was sleeping."

We had already left him
when I saw two frozen in one hole,
so that one's head was a hat for the other;

and as bread is devoured by the hungry,
so the one on top put his teeth into the other
there where the brain joins the neck:

not otherwise did Tydeus chew on
Melanippus's temples out of disdain
than this guy did to the skull and other things.

"Hey you who show by such a bestial sign
hatred for that guy you're eating,
tell me why," I said, "with this agreement,

if you have good reason to resent him:
knowing who you two are and what his sin is,
I can still clear your name in the world up there,
if my ability to speak doesn't dry up."

Canto XXXIII

The mouth raised from the ferocious meal
of the sinner, wiping it clean on the hair
of the man's head he'd been laying to waste.

Then he began: "You want me to renew
the desperate pain my heart feels
already just thinking about it, before I tell you about it.

But if my words might be seeds
that bear the fruit of the infamy of the traitor I'm
devouring,
you'll see me speak and weep together.

I don't know who you are nor how
you have come down here; but
you really seem to be from Florence, when I hear you
speak.

You need to know that I was Count Ugolino;
this was Archbishop Ruggieri:
now I'll tell you why I'm such a neighbor to him.

So to achieve his evil plans,
getting me to trust him, I was taken
and then put to death, no need to talk about it;

but what you can't have heard about
is how cruel my death was;
you'll hear and know if he has done me wrong.

A little gap inside the wall of the cell

which because of me has the title 'Hunger,'
and where others still will be shut in,

had shown me through its opening
one moon after another, when I had the nightmare
of the future that tore the veil.

This one appeared to me as lord and master
hunting the wolf and whelps in the mountain
that hides Lucca from the people of Pisa,

along with lean dogs, intent and intense,
Gualandi with Sismondi and with Lanfranchi
he'd put at the very front.

After a little chase, they seemed tired,
father and sons, and with sharp fangs
it seemed to me I saw their flanks shredded.

When I woke before the start of the next day,
I heard the sound of my little sons
crying there with me, asking for bread.

You are quite cruel if you aren't already weeping,
thinking of what my heart said to me;
and if you don't cry, what does make you cry?

They were already awake, and the hour approached
when food was usually brought to us,
and each was in doubt because of his dream;

and I heard them shutting the exit below
to the horrible tower; I looked

wordlessly into the faces of my sons.

I wasn't crying, so had I turned to stone inside;
they were crying, and my little Anselm
said: 'You have such a look, father! What's wrong with
you?'

Even so, I didn't weep and neither did I speak
all that day nor the next night,
until the next day's sun came out into the world.

As a little ray came
into the sorrowful prison, and I made out
the four little faces that had my own expression,

I bit both my hands in grief;
and they, thinking I was doing this from the need
to eat, suddenly got up

and said: 'Father, it would be less painful
if you eat us: you clothed us
with this miserable flesh, and you take it off.'

Then I quieted myself so I wouldn't make them sadder;
that day and the next we all stayed silent;
oh cruel earth, why didn't you open?

When we'd all made it to the fourth day,
Gaddo threw himself at my feet,
saying: 'My father, why don't you help me?'

Then he died; and as you see me,
I saw all three fall there one by one

the fifth day and sixth; when I,

already blind, crawled over each one,
and for two days called to them, though they werc dead.
Then, what sorrow could not do, fasting did."

When he'd said this, with his eyes distorted,
he clamped the miserable skull again in his teeth,
like a bone to a dog, ravenously.

Pisa, shame of the people
of the beautiful country there where the "Sì" resounds,
since your neighbors are slow to punish you,

may Capraia and Gorgona
dam up the Arno River's mouth
and drown everyone in you!

If Count Ugolino was said
to have betrayed your castles,
you shouldn't have crucified his children like that.

Their young age made them innocent,
new Thebes, little Ugi and the Brig,
and the other two that my song named above.

We went on, to where the ice
roughly wraps another group of people,
not turned down, but reversed.

Crying itself there doesn't let them cry,
and the pain that finds its way blocked from the eyes
turns inward to grow distress;

205

so the tears first make a cluster,
and so, like a crystal visor,
refill the cup under the eyebrow.

And though, like a callus,
the cold sent all feeling
from my face,

still I seemed to feel a wind;
so I said: "My teacher, who is moving this?
Isn't every vapor down here stilled?"

And he to me: "You will soon be where
your eyes will have the answer,
seeing the cause that makes a deluge of the blast."

One of the sad ones in the cold crust
shouted at us: "Souls so cruel
that you've been sent to the last post,

lift from my face these hard veils
so I can free myself of the pain that impregnates my heart
a little, before crying freezes them again."

So I said to him: "If you want me to help you,
tell me who you are; then if I don't free you,
may I have to go to the very bottom of the ice."

He responded then: "I am Brother Alberigo;
I am he of the fruit of the evil orchard,
and here I am repaid dates for figs."

"Oh," I said to him, "are you already dead?"
And he to me: "How my body is making out
in the world above, I know nothing.

Such advantage Ptolemea has,
that many times a soul falls here
before Atropos moves it.

And so that you may all the more willingly clear my
glassy tears from my face,
know that, as soon as the soul betrays,

as I did, his body is taken
by a demon, who then rules it
while its time unwinds.

It falls into this cesspool;
and maybe the body still appears, above,
of the shadow wintering here behind me.

You must know about these, if you've just come down;
he is Mister Branca Doria, and it's many years
since he was locked up."

"I believe," I said to him, "that you're tricking me;
that Branca Doria is not at all dead yet,
and he eats and drinks and sleeps and dresses still."

"In the ditch up there," he said, "of The Evil Claws,
there where the tenacious pitch boils,
Michel Zanche hadn't gotten there yet,

so this guy left a devil in his stead

in his body, and one of his close relatives
who'd committed treason together with him.

But reach your hand down here;
open my eyes." And I didn't open them;
and it was a courtesy to him to be so rude.

Genovese, different men
of every custom and full of every evildoing,
why aren't you exiled from the world?

With the most evil spirit of Romagna
I found one such of you who by his works
already bathes his soul in Cocytus, the Lake of
Lamentation,
and still appears alive in his body, up above.

Canto XXXIV

"'The banners of the king' of Hell advance
toward us; so look ahead,"
said my teacher, "and see if you can see him."

As when a thick fog rises,
or when night blackens our hemisphere,
far away the wind turns a windmill:

it seemed to me I saw something like that;
then the wind made me pull back behind
my guide, as there was no other sanctuary.

Now I was, and with fear I put it in my verse,
there where all the spirits were covered
and showed through like straw in glass.

Some lie down; others stand erect,
that with the head and that with the soles of the feet;
another, like an arc, face inverted to feet.

When we were far enough ahead
that my teacher was pleased to show me
the creature who had once seemed so beautiful,

he stepped from in front of me and made me stop:
"This is Dis, Ruler of the Underworld," saying, "and this
is the place
where you must arm yourself with strength."

How I then became frozen and weak,
don't ask, reader, as I won't write it,

because to speak at all would be insufficient.

I didn't die, and I didn't go on living;
think for yourself, if it isn't beyond your genius,
what I became, deprived of one and the other.

The emperor of the kingdom of sorrow
rose out of the ice from the middle of his chest;
and I am closer in size to a giant,

than giants would be measured against his arms:
you see how much must be the whole
that is so made in part.

If he was once as beautiful as he now is ugly,
and raised his brow against his maker,
it well may be that from him proceeds every struggle.

Oh, how much it appeared to me a marvel
when I saw three faces on his head!
One in front, and that was quite red;

there were two others that joined this one
over the middle of each shoulder,
and all joined at the top of his head:

the right appeared white and yellow;
the left seemed like those
who come from where the Nile falls.

Under each stuck out two great wings,
as great as would be needed for such a bird:
I've never seen ships' sails like these.

There were no feathers, but like a bat's
they were made; and when these waved,
it was as if three winds moved from him:

that's why Cocytus, Lake of Lamentation, was congealed.
With his six eyes he wept, and from three chins
he dripped tears and bloody drool.

At each mouth he chewed with his teeth
a sinner, like a grinder,
so that three of them suffered.

For the one in front, the biting was nothing
compared to the clawing, so that sometimes the spine
was raked clean of skin.

"That soul up there most in pain,"
said the teacher, "is Judas Iscariot,
who has his head inside, and outside hang his legs.

Of the other two who have their heads hanging down,
that one hanging from the black snout is Brutus:
see how he contorts himself and doesn't say a word!

And the other is Cassius, who seems so lanky.
But night is rising, and it's time
to depart, because we've seen it all."

As he wanted, I held onto his neck;
and he chose the time and place,
and when the wings opened wide enough,

he grabbed a fistful of the hairy sides;
then from handful to handful down he descended
between the thick fur and the crusts of ice.

When we were there where the thigh
turns, at the point on the big part of the hip,
the guide, tired and anguished,

turned his head where he had his legs,
and grabbed the hair like a man who's climbing up,
so that I thought we were returning again to Hell.

"Hold on well, for by such stairs,"
said the teacher, breathing like an exhausted man,
"we need to depart from so much evil."

Then he came out through an opening in the rock
and put me up on its edge to sit;
then he came close to me with short steps.

I raised my eyes and thought I would see
Lucifer as I'd left him,
and saw him with his legs held up;

and if I then became agitated,
let gross people think about it, who don't see
what and what point I had passed.

"Get up," said the teacher, "on your feet:
the road is long and the way is evil,
and already the sun returns to the middle third of the sky."

It was not the walkway of a palace

there where we were, but a natural dungeon
that had a bad floor and weak light.

"Before I pry myself from the abyss,
my teacher," I said when I was upright,
"bring me away from error with a few words:

where is the ice? And this one, how is he fixed
so, upside-down? And how, in such a short time,
from the evening, has the sun made its trajectory?"

And he to me: "You still imagine
being there beyond the center, where I took hold
of the hair of the foul worm that runs through the world.

You were beyond there as long as I went down;
when I turned, you passed the point
at which weights are dragged from every side.

And now you are below the hemisphere that reaches
opposite the one the great dryness covers,
and under that where ended

the life of the man who was born and lived without sin;
you have your feet on a little sphere
that makes the other face of Judecca.

Here it is day when there it is evening;
and this one, whose skin we made stairs of,
is still fixed as he was before.

Here he fell down from Heaven;
and the earth, that before was spread out here,

for fear of him veiled itself under the sea,

and became our hemisphere; and maybe
to flee him left this place empty when
what had appeared there, ran back up."

There is a place down there far from The Lord of the
Flies,
as far as a tomb can stretch,
that can't be found by sight but by the sound

of a stream that descends
through a hole in the stone that it has cut
with its current turning and softly sloping down.

The guide and I by that hidden way
entered to return to the clear world;
and without concern for a moment's rest,

we came up, he first and I second,
so that I saw the beautiful things
that Heaven brings, through the round crevice.
And then we came out to see again the stars.

THE END